HOMELESS STALKER

Is an obsession to seek revenge at any price, worth it?

GLENN PARKER

The Homeless Stalker
Copyright © 2017 by Glenn Parker

No part of this publication may be reproduced, distributed, or transmitted in any form or by any means, including photocopying, recording, or other electronic or mechanical methods, without the prior written permission of the author, except in the case of brief quotations embodied in critical reviews and certain other non-commercial uses permitted by copyright law.

Tellwell Talent
www.tellwell.ca

ISBN
978-1-77370-197-4 (Paperback)
978-1-77370-196-7 (eBook)

OTHER BOOKS BY GLENN PARKER:

The Shutout Girl

The Littlest Hockey Player

Hockey Fever

The Lonely Little Leaguer

The Trouble with Tommy

Fatal Distraction

DEDICATION

To all women, as well as men, who have been either stalked or abused by a loved one, I dedicate this novel. Anyone in this position has had their life so badly affected, that living any kind of normal life is almost impossible. It is a sad state of affairs that stalking and abuse goes on despite all the negative publicity it has received over many years. My heart goes out to anyone who has had to endure a spouse or loved one or perhaps a complete stranger who has systematically made someone's life unendurable.

CHAPTER ONE

JANET MORRISON LOOKED OVER AT THE MAN LYING ON the bed, passed out from drinking too many beers and now making strange-sounding wheezes as though he was about to pass over into the next world. She wished with all her heart that he would die right where he was. That would save her having to do what she knew she had to do.

How had it all come to this? How had she found herself in this seedy motel room when she should have been at home looking after her fifteen-year-old son and living a decent life? Running out on him and leaving him to his own devises was something she would never have imagined. And she wouldn't have done it if it wasn't for the drunk who was spread-eagled on the bed.

Ross McDonald.

She was convinced that he was a sociopath. Why else would he be acting the way he had been for the last year? At one time, Janet had been dazzled by his good looks and outgoing personality and he seemed to be the man she was looking for after her husband had been killed in a car accident. She was only in her thirties, surely not too old to hope for a new life with a man who could accept her son, make her happy and provide a home for them.

But that hadn't happened. Ross McDonald turned out to be a possessive, egotistical tyrant who, shortly after moving in with her, made her life so miserable that she seemed incapable by any means of getting her old life back, unexciting as it was. Oh, he was a charmer all right and said all the right things, bought her flowers and flattered her. He even seemed to like her son, Andrew. But all that disappeared within weeks of his moving in with her and now what was she supposed to do? How do you get rid of someone you're not only afraid of, but who has wormed himself into your life and virtually taken over?

Janet did not have anybody she could talk to except her son and what could a fifteen-year-old do to help her anyway? Besides, from the outside, it looked like everything was perfect. Ross worked regularly and brought home a paycheck of which she never saw a penny. He never gave her any money for anything despite the fact that there were a lot of expenses. What did he do with his money? She hadn't any idea.

When they had first met, Janet worked as a waitress in one of the nicest restaurants in the area. She made good money from tips and enjoyed her job. Everybody liked her. But it wasn't long before Ross decided that he didn't want her working any more. He had come into the restaurant on several occasions and didn't like the way some of the customers looked at her.

"It's no wonder guys leer at you and undress you in their minds with those skimpy outfits you wear," he complained

Now he had decided that he had had enough of living in an old house with scarcely enough room for two people, let alone three. The house sat on four acres of scrub pine and couch grass. The whole place needed a lot of work, but Ross never lifted a hand to do anything to clean the place up and make it look respectable. That would have been beneath him. He much preferred to bring home a dozen beer and park himself in front of the TV and watch violent cop shows. Janet didn't dare say anything. Ross had a hair-spring temper and wouldn't hesitate to slap her around if she questioned anything he did. He had already shown that he didn't mind using his fists to keep her in line. When her son Andrew had asked her about the bruises, she had had to lie to him. Whether he believed her, she wasn't sure. She hated lying to her son, but she was afraid that if he knew the truth, he might confront Ross and that would make everything even worse.

When he informed her that they were moving, Janet was speechless. Where were they going and why? She had always lived here. This was her home, even though the house they lived in was a rental and hardly what anybody would consider a nice place to live. But it was familiar and in the country and Janet didn't have to bother about neighbors. And she could wander around enjoying the wild flowers, the hedgerow and the slow- moving creek that meandered through the property.

However, when Ross told her that it was only going to be the two of them moving, that her son Andrew was just going to have to fend for himself, Janet couldn't believe what she was hearing. There was no way she was leaving without her son.

"The kid's old enough to look after himself," Ross said. "He's almost sixteen for heaven's sake. When I was sixteen I was earning good money and doing the work of a man."

"He's still in school," Janet said. "He's a promising student. I've got plans for him."

Ross laughed. "He's a wimp and he's never done a day's work in his life. And what kind of plans do you have for him? You don't have a cent to your name. If you're thinking of sending him to college, where are you going to get the money? Not from me, that's for sure."

"There are scholarships. He's a very good student you know."

"Yeah, I'll bet he is. You want to turn him into a book worm. If he was my son, I'd make a man out of him. But he's not mine thank heavens."

"I'm not going anywhere without him," Janet protested.

"Is that right." Ross grabbed her and threw her to the floor. "You just listen here little missy. When I tell you we're moving and we're not taking that useless son of yours, I mean it. So, start packing." He waved a fist in front of her face. "You can either do that or face the consequences and they won't be nice."

After forcing her out the door and into his car before she had even packed enough clothes and personal items to last her a few days, Ross pealed out of the yard and headed down the road.

Janet couldn't help wondering why he was in such a hurry to leave. Were the cops after him? She had always wondered whether he was involved in selling drugs or some other illicit business, but she hadn't paid much attention to what he did when he left the house on the odd occasion in the evening.

Janet left sixty dollars for Andrew when Ross wasn't looking. She tucked it down inside his bedsheet so he was certain to see it when he went to bed. If Ross had known she had done that, he would have taken the money himself and probably struck her. She knew she was taking a chance, but she wasn't about to leave Andrew with no money. Where was he going to get his next meal? There was nothing in the fridge.

She looked at Ross as he wheezed and snorted and thought about how much she hated him, hated the way he had treated her in the last few years. How would she rid herself of him? If she were to just drive away, he would find her and things would be even worse for her than they were now.

She glanced around the motel room, but there wasn't anything she could use to dispatch him. Nothing heavy enough or sharp enough. Could she kill him in cold blood? She had thought about it often enough, but the thought of not being successful scared her. There was no doubt that Ross would severely brutalize her if she tried to kill him and was unsuccessful.

She went to the window and looked out. There had to be an answer to her problem short of murder, but she didn't know what it was. She didn't have any big brothers or a father who could threaten Ross, run him off, warn him to stay away from her unless he wanted to suffer the consequences.

She opened the door and looked out. Freedom. Oh, how she longed for it. And she already missed Andrew. When would she him again, she wondered? She could have phoned him but Ross had made sure she didn't have a phone. He had told her that owning a phone was like being chained to other people and always having to worry about whether she had missed a call or needed to look up some useless information that would only make her more dependent than she already was.

Her eyes fell on the rockery and the beautiful flowers within its border. She walked toward it, leaned down and picked up one of the rocks. It was extremely heavy and she swayed trying to keep her balance holding onto it.

She was almost laughing when she returned to the interior of the motel, staggered over to where Ross lay stretched out on the bed and held the rock over his head. She was sure she couldn't do it. She was many things, but she wasn't a …murderer.

Or was she?

She held the rock as high as she could and still hold onto it, and then let it drop. She heard the crunching sound as it struck Ross a direct hit on his face. There was a lack of sound as the wheezing ceased and it was suddenly quiet in the room. She couldn't bear to look at what destruction she had wreaked. She was certain she had killed him. There just was no way he could survive being hit by a rock of that size.

For several seconds she was so dazed at what she had just done, that she couldn't move. Then, in a flurry of motion, she grabbed her coat and purse and fled out the door. In her hurry to get away, she almost hit another car. As she gained control and was finally looking at the motel in her rearview mirror, she began to breathe normally.

Had she really killed the man who had made her life unbearable these past few years? If she were caught, she could plead self-defense, couldn't she? Or better still, justifiable homicide. Once they heard how he had mistreated her, surely they would show sympathy and agree that she had done the right thing, the only thing open to her.

Wayne Allison sat on the side of his bed looking out at the blackness of the night. It was two o'clock in the morning and he couldn't sleep. What could possibly be on the mind of a fifteen-year-old that was so important that it kept him from sleeping? He had it made as far as his life was concerned. He had two great parents. His dad was a science teacher at another school. His mom used to be a nurse, but she gave that up when Wayne came along and hadn't returned to it yet. She kept talking about going back to work, but nothing had materialized so far. It was kind of nice having his mom around when he got home from school. She did a lot of volunteering. She had to be the champion volunteer of the whole city. And she loved to organize things for the neighborhood like family get togethers, picnics, golf tournaments, trail walks. That kind of stuff. She had lots of energy.

Being an only child as far as Wayne was concerned was the greatest thing since sliced bread. You hear so much about how only children are spoiled and don't develop good social relationships and all that stuff. Hey, maybe that's why he was so weird. Who knew. On the other hand, it would be great to have a brother to bounce things off, talk things over with. Of course, you can't always order up a brother who will end up being your friend and help you out with your thinking and that sort of thing. But one can always dream.

The nice thing about his parents was that they weren't big time into parenting. They pretty much let him do whatever he wanted to do. They weren't always dropping things on him like, "Wayne, you should study harder so you can become an accountant or a dentist or an undertaker or something thrilling like that." What he would really like to be was an actor, but everybody told him there was no money in that unless you were discovered by Hollywood. Not that he particularly wanted to be rich and famous when he grew up, but it would be nice to be comfortable. Maybe about like his parents.

After discovering that he couldn't get back to sleep no matter what he did, he began to wonder what it was like outside at two o'clock in the morning, not having had that experience. So, after getting dressed, he opened the basement window and out he climbed. It seemed really weird being outside when he should have been sound asleep, but he was strangely enjoying the sensation. His parents would probably have been quite concerned having their only child wandering around at two a.m., but he felt a freedom that was quite refreshing.

Their house wasn't far from the water, so he made his way down the hillside and sat on a big rock that overlooked the bay. There was a full moon and he had a perfect view of everything. The town sat twinkling in the distance and everything seemed somewhat unreal as though he was looking at a painting. He sat there feeling perfectly comfortable just taking in the beautiful panorama when he heard a noise. If it hadn't been for the full moon, he would never have seen this guy as he crawled out of a flattened box not fifty feet away and began looking around. When he finally spied Wayne sitting on the rock, he gave him a wave. Of course, Wayne waved back. How often do you see somebody at 2 o'clock in the morning sitting on an empty box? Of course, he waved back. It would have been the ultimate in rudeness not to.

He looked about Wayne's age, but what was he doing here? Was he homeless? He seemed to be a little young for that. Maybe he was having some sort of dispute with his parents and had run off. Wayne had heard of that happening often enough. Or maybe he was hiding from the police. That gave him a little pause.

After they stared at one another for several minutes and Wayne's curiosity got the better of him, he wandered over. The guy looked harmless enough. Wayne wasn't particularly concerned that the young man was about to attack him or pose a threat of any kind. And when he stood up, he could see that he wasn't any bigger than Wayne.

"How's it going?" Wayne said, as he approached him. Obviously, it wasn't going very well considering he was sleeping inside an empty box. When Wayne got right up to him, he suddenly recognized him. He was the new student who had appeared in his classroom that day.

"Okay, I guess," he said, in a squeaky voice.

"Do you live around here?" Wayne asked.

"Not really." He gestured toward the box he had crawled out from. "This is where I live now. I dragged it here from the back of the 7/11 down the road a piece."

"Oh. Not exactly the Ritz huh?"

"Not exactly," he said, giving a little chuckle. His whole face lit up when he smiled.

"Where are your parents?"

He shrugged. "Don't know. They could be in Timbuktu for all I know."

Wow, Wayne thought, trying to get his mind around the fact that this guy didn't even know where his parents were. How did that happen? He couldn't imagine how he would feel if his parents suddenly disappeared from his life.

"They just left," he explained. "I found sixty dollars on my bed. I guess they didn't want me to starve over the next few days. Not even a note to say goodbye and good luck and that they hoped everything would work out for me. I guess that would have been too much to hope for all things considered."

"Holy crap. Really? Your parents must be..." He wanted to say something like cruel or thoughtless or selfish, but he thought better of it. The guy probably already felt bad enough about his parents without Wayne adding to it. "I'm sorry to hear that."

He shrugged. "My dad died a few years ago. My mom's boyfriend was my substitute dad, but he didn't exactly enjoy his role. He was pretty mean to my mom too. She ended up with a shiner or two and tried to convince me that she had just bumped her head or something." He chuckled again, looking thoughtful. "I would like to have knocked his lights out, but I knew I was no match for him. It's no exaggeration that we didn't see eye to eye on most things."

Wayne recalled when he had entered their class room and the teacher had introduced him. He had looked pretty shabby then, his clothes obviously hadn't been washed for several weeks and he gave off an odor that caused several students to move away from him. He probably hadn't had a shower for a week or more. He was somewhat comical looking with big ears and bright blue eyes and a snub nose. His hair, a dark brown, stuck out in every direction. He remembered feeling kind of sorry for him, not only for the way the other students stared at him as though he was something that had crawled out from under a rock, but because he looked so neglected. Now he knew why.

Wayne approached him and held out his hand. "I'm Wayne, Wayne Allison. I live in that house with the fir trees surrounding it," he added, pointing at their house.

"Nice place," the fellow said, taking Wayne's hand. "I'm Andy Morrison. And this is my house," he added, pointing to his cardboard box. "It's not much, but it's all I got and there's no mortgage."

"Doesn't it get cold out here sleeping in a cardboard box?"

"I got some blankets in there and some extra clothes. But you get used to it. I guess a person can get used to anything if they have to."

Wayne sat down on a log and looked over toward his own house. What a contrast and how privileged was he to be living in such comfort compared to his new acquaintance. "How long have you been living here?"

Andy sat down on his cardboard box and sighed. "Hmm. I guess about a few weeks. I don't know. It seems longer but you kind of lose track of time when you live like this. And it gets pretty boring after a while. Sometimes I think I'm going to go bonkers. And I sure would like to have a shower. You get a little grubby when you don't have any hot water or cold water for that matter."

Wayne thought about Andy and his situation. It wasn't fair that life had treated him so poorly. What had he done to deserve such an existence? It was all a matter of luck, he decided. In Andy's case, having a mother who cared more about her boyfriend than her son was hard to get his mind around. He couldn't imagine his mom leaving him and running off with someone. It just wasn't possible as far as he was concerned and it would never have entered his head that such a thing could ever take place.

"You can't stay here forever," Wayne told him. "You could die out here."

"Yeah, I know." He shrugged. "Guess I'm going to have to come up with Plan B whatever that is."

Wayne had to get back to his house and his warm bed. He had things to do tomorrow and if he didn't get his sleep, he wasn't going to be any good to anybody. But he couldn't just walk away from Andy knowing that all he had was a cardboard box to crawl back into.

"Why don't you come over to my place?" he finally offered. "You could take a shower and you could get out of those old clothes. We're about the same size. I got lots of clothes and we've got an extra bed you could sleep in."

Andy just stared at him for several seconds, his mouth slightly open as though he couldn't quite believe what Wayne was saying. "That would be great…but what would your parents say?"

"They wouldn't mind. My parents are very open-minded. I'm sure they would understand." He wasn't quite sure they would, but there was no way he was going to leave Andy and walk back to his warm bed and comfortable existence knowing Andy was out here in the elements practically freezing.

Andy stood up and gave his cardboard box a kick. "I'm not sure why you're doing this, but I'm not about to look a gift horse in the mouth."

"Then it's settled." Wayne started walking back toward his house with Andy following him. He felt good that he had made the right decision. He didn't know much about his newfound friend, but from what he had said, he deserved a break and Wayne was about to give him one. Besides, he was beginning to like him.

CHAPTER TWO

As they approached his window, Wayne turned and explained to Andy that his window was really a door and that he used it so he wouldn't wake up his parents.

"They don't know that I've taken to prowling around at 2 o'clock in the morning."

Andy laughed. "I couldn't count the number of times I jumped out of my window, but I didn't do it because I was afraid of waking up my parents. They probably couldn't have cared less. It was just easier to go out the window than walking through the house and out the front door."

Wayne went in first and then gave Andy a hand. When he turned on the light, Andy looked surprised. "Wow. Nice pad. You ought to see my bedroom. It's pretty bad. I mean really bad. And it wasn't a bedroom anyway. It was the living room with a foamy. Of course, I don't have it any more, but maybe that's a blessing."

Wayne gestured toward the hide-a-bed that sat against the wall. "You can sleep on that. It makes into a bed. I think it's fairly comfortable, but I've never slept on it, so you'll have to take my word for it."

"It's got to be a lot more comfortable than the inside of a cardboard box. And a lot warmer too."

"You've got a point there," Wayne said, smiling and feeling good that he was able to rescue Andy from his cardboard box.

Wayne tiptoed into the hallway where the linen closet was and pulled out some sheets and pillow cases as well as a comforter. Together, he and Andy tugged on the couch until it flattened out into a bed. Then they proceeded to apply the sheets. Since Wayne had two pillows on his bed, he gave one to Andy. He had never quite figured out why his mom thought he needed two pillows anyway.

After they had made the bed, Andy seemed a little bewildered and stood looking around until Wayne figured out that the poor guy needed loungers. He couldn't very well sleep in his dirty clothes. And Wayne was pretty sure he didn't want to shuck them off in front of him.

"I'll get you a pair of loungers," he said, going over to his dresser and hauling out a fresh pair. He tossed them over to Andy and pointed to his bathroom. "You can change in there."

"Could I take a shower first?" Andy inquired. "I'm pretty dirty. In fact, I'm downright filthy."

Wayne knocked himself on the head. How could he have been so stupid? Of course he would want a shower after being out in the elements for two weeks and not having any access to warm water.

"Wayne went into the bathroom and found a clean towel and handed it to him. Andy looked relieved.

"You don't know how I've looked forward to having a shower," he said. "It's going to be a little like being in heaven."

"Go for it," Wayne told him. "You deserve it."

He got into bed and stared up at the ceiling, feeling good about himself and enjoying Andy's company. Maybe this was what it was like having a brother, something he had thought a lot about over his fifteen years.

Ten minutes later, Andy came out wearing Wayne's loungers and looking like a totally different person. Wayne could hardly believe the transformation.

"Hey, who is this guy coming out of my bathroom? Did you perform some kind of magic trick while you were in there?"

Andy laughed. "I feel like a new person. It's like I shed an old skin... a really old smelly skin."

It didn't take Andy long to get to sleep. In fact, Wayne was sure that Andy was sound asleep by the time his head hit the pillow. But he was still wide awake.

Wasn't this where he came in?

He lay wondering about what his parents would think about inviting a complete stranger into his room and offering him a bed. Nice gesture but what did he really know about Andy? Only what he had told him and who was to say he was telling him the truth? He sighed. Andy struck him as being an honest person, somebody who wouldn't be pulling the wool over his eyes. He was quite sure that his assessment of people was sufficient to sense that.

He didn't know how long he lay counting the squares in the ceiling panel, but it seemed a long time. He must have dropped off at some point, because the next thing he heard was his mom telling him it was time to get up.

He looked over at Andy and he was still dead to the world. He probably hadn't had a good sleep for two weeks and was making up for lost time. Wayne got up and went into the bathroom, being careful not to wake Andy up. The poor guy needed his sleep. As far as Wayne was concerned, he could sleep in all day if he wanted. After all, it was Saturday and they didn't have to rush off to school.

When he came out of the bathroom, however, Andy was sitting on the side of his bed, looking a little sleepy and probably wondering what was coming next.

"Good morning," Wayne said.

"Good morning. Haven't had a sleep like that since I was two years old." He chuckled. "There just ain't nothing like a good night's rest even though it was only about five hours. I don't think I got more than an hour or two at a time when I was outside."

"You don't have to get up," Wayne told him. "Stay in bed. You probably need a few more hours anyway."

Andy yawned. "Maybe you're right." He fell back on the bed and pulled the covers over himself. Then he peeked out. "You sure it's going to be okay? I don't want you to get in trouble with your parents."

"Don't you worry about that. I'll take care of my parents. They're pretty understanding."

When he went into the kitchen, his mom was making breakfast and his dad was reading the newspaper in the living room.

"Did you have a shower last night?" his mom asked. "I thought I heard the water running."

"Ah…no, not exactly."

His Mom laughed. "Now what does that mean? Either you had a shower or you didn't."

"My guest had a shower," he said. There was no point in beating around the bush about it. He had always been open and honest with his parents. He might as well find out sooner rather than later, what they thought about him having a guest.

"I beg your pardon? A guest? Now who might that be?"

"His name's Andy. He's in my class at school and he's a really nice guy. You'll like him."

Mom stood with her hands on her hips. "Wayne, you're not making much sense. As far as I know, when you went to bed last night, you were by yourself. When did this so-called "guest" arrive?"

"About two-thirty a.m.," he said. He shrugged and tried his best to look nonchalant as though having a friend come over in the small hours of the morning was nothing out of the ordinary. His mom wasn't buying it.

"I think you had better sit down and tell me the whole story," she said.

They sat across from one another. Wayne was having difficulty meeting her inquisitive gaze. She must have thought he had lost his mind. He gave her a lopsided grin. "There isn't much to tell really. I was out by the cliffs enjoying the night air and…"

"What in the world were you doing out there in the middle of the night?"

"I couldn't sleep so I crawled out the window and I figured if I got a little bit of fresh air, it might help me to sleep."

"And this friend of yours just happened along?" She looked at Wayne doubtfully.

"Actually, he was sleeping about twenty yards away from me inside a cardboard box. I thought he was a homeless person or something until he crawled out and I recognized him."

"This is getting curioser and curioser by the minute. If you weren't my very own son, I would think you were hallucinating." She began to laugh. "Wayne, are you going to tell me that this…this guest is sleeping in your room at this very minute?"

When he nodded, she shook her head. "I can hardly wait to meet him. He must be an extraordinary human being."

"He's okay. I don't think he's extraordinary though."

"Now you just let me be the judge of that," his mom said. "I'm a very good judge of character as you well know."

He didn't know that, but he let it pass. His mom was a great person, very open-minded, kind and accepting, but he hadn't thought about her being a good judge of character. But he guessed she was. She was good at everything else so why wouldn't she be a good judge of character?

"So, what was he doing inside a cardboard box?" she wanted to know.

"Trying to sleep I guess."

His mom glared at Wayne. "Don't be a smarty pants with me young man. You know perfectly well what I mean."

"His mom and dad, step-dad or whatever he is, deserted him. Just walked away leaving him to fend for himself. Nice huh?"

"So, you, being the wonderful human being that you are, offered him a bed for the night." When Wayne nodded, she came around the table and put her arms around him. "I'm so proud of you, son. No mother could be prouder. That was a wonderful thing for you to do."

His mom was always so complimentary. Sometimes he wondered what he had done to deserve such a great mom.

"I guess I should wake him up."

"No...no, let him sleep. The poor guy is probably sleep-deprived if he's been sleeping outside in a cardboard box."

His dad came into the kitchen. "Good morning, Wayne. What are you two hatching out here this fine morning?"

His dad was an optimist, always in a good mood, nothing seemed to bother him very much. That was probably why he was such a good teacher.

"Wayne has a guest," Mrs. Allison announced.

"Really? Well, where is he? And how come I didn't know about this?"

"He's still sleeping," Wayne said. "I think he's pretty tired."

Mr. Allison looked at his wife and then back at Wayne. He looked thoroughly confused. "Am I missing something here?"

Wayne shrugged. "My guest is...a homeless teenager, Dad. His parents ran out on him."

"Well, that certainly explains everything. And you stepped in and adopted him. Is that it?"

Wayne had to laugh. His dad could be quite funny at times.

"He's in Wayne's class at school," Mrs. Allison explained. "He's been sleeping outside for the last few weeks, inside a cardboard box, if you can imagine that."

"Not having had that experience, I can't imagine it. But it doesn't sound very...desirable. In fact, it sounds downright depressing. How did you happen to run across him?"

"His cardboard box was quite close to where I was...resting."

"Resting?" his dad quizzed. "You've found a new outside bedroom, have you?"

Wayne laughed. "No, not really. I was just- "

At that moment, the basement door opened and Andy stepped in and approached the kitchen looking a little sleepy. "Good morning," he said. "I hope I'm not interrupting anything."

"Not at all," Mr. Allison said. "Come and join us for breakfast. We were just having a conversation about adoption."

"Oh? Well, I guess I should get dressed first. But I-"

Wayne jumped up and approached him. "I'm sorry, Andy. I forgot to get out some clothes for you." He turned back to his parents. "I'll just dig out something for him to wear. We'll just be a minute."

They walked back down the stairs and into Wayne's bedroom. Wayne took a dressing gown off the hook on the door and handed it to Andy. "Here, why don't you wear this. I never wear it myself and we can get out some clothes for you later."

"Thanks," he said, taking the dressing gown and putting it on over his loungers. "I almost feel like somebody important wearing this. It's very nice."

"You are somebody important," Wayne told him.

He laughed. "Yeah, I'm the exclusive owner of a large cardboard box and a bunch of old clothes." He bowed. "And I can grant you any wish you desire."

Maybe Andy was extraordinary like Mom said. He certainly had an original way of expressing himself.

"My parents are anxious to meet you. And you must be starved."

"My sixty dollars ran out a long time ago, but I needed to go on a diet anyway."

Wayne laughed. If there was one thing Andy didn't need it was to go on a diet.

When they re-entered the kitchen, Wayne's mom rushed over and gave Andy a hug. "Welcome to our home," she said. "I hope you slept all right."

"Like a log," Andy said. "Best sleep I've had since I was a baby."

"Well, you must be really hungry," Mrs. Allison said. "You just sit right down here and I'll get you something to eat."

Mr. Allison held out his hand. "I'm Wayne's dad," he said. "Make yourself at home. We're pretty casual around here."

"What do you usually have for breakfast?" Wayne's mom asked him. "We've got cereal, toast, eggs. You just name it and it's yours."

Andy shrugged. "Anything edible will do. My diet lately hasn't exactly been nourishing. In fact, it has been downright awful. It's amazing what these restaurants throw away. You could feed half the people in Asia with what they toss out."

Wayne's mom made a face. Wayne could just imagine what she thought of eating food thrown out by a restaurant. She poured him a bowlful of cereal and set it down in front of him. "You can get started on that. I'll just whip up some scrambled eggs."

"What are your plans?" Wayne's dad asked as Andy poured milk on his cereal. "I hope your cardboard box can be laid to rest." He looked over at Wayne. "Maybe we can use it to start a bonfire in the back yard. What do you think, Wayne?"

Wayne laughed. It was so like his dad to say something like that. "Sounds like a good idea to me."

"My plans?" Andy said, looking thoughtful. "Hmm. Survival I suppose. And a warm bed. When you're in my position there aren't many options."

"You could stay here," Wayne said. "We've got lots of room and if you can stand that hide-a-bed to sleep on."

Andy looked a little dumbfounded. "I...I'm not sure I could do that. I mean, you hardly know me. I could be a sociopath or an arsonist anxious to burn your house down and run off with your prize possessions."

Wayne's mom laughed. "Somehow I don't think we need to worry about that."

Mr. Allison looked over at her. "Andy's right. We don't know anything about you, but there are some things you have to take on faith. You look like a nice young man," he continued, smiling over at Andy, "but sometimes appearances are deceptive. Perhaps today we can do a little…looking into things, find out what has occurred in your life and what your options are. Does that sound reasonable?"

"It does. Where do we start?" Andy asked. "All my stuff is still in our house, or at least the house my mom was renting. I wouldn't mind getting it back."

"Well, there's a place to start," Mr. Allison said. "We can take a ride over there and see if we can retrieve your belongings."

Andy looked relieved.

CHAPTER THREE

After Wayne produced a pair of jeans and a t-shirt as well as a pair of shoes that were a little big for him, Andy stood in the middle of the room looking like an entirely new person. His wide grin confirmed that he felt completely at home. If their positions had been reversed, Wayne didn't know if he would have felt the way Andy was obviously feeling. Andy seemed to be fitting right into their family which was remarkable in itself. He seemed very unself-conscious as though this was his life and he was accepting it for whatever it threw at him.

On the way over to his former house, Andy briefly outlined his life. He was fifteen years old, the same age as Wayne, he had always been quite close to his mother until Ross, her current boyfriend, had entered the picture and then things had changed. On the surface, Ross seemed like a likable enough guy, but as time went on, his true colors began to show.

"He treated my mom very badly," Andy said. "He even punched her a few times and gave her a black eye. If I had been there at the time, I might have been able to protect her, but maybe not. Ross is bigger than me and is always pumping iron. He's in great shape so he wouldn't have much trouble with a shrimp like me."

Wayne shook his head. He couldn't imagine his dad punching his mom. And if he did, he wasn't sure what he would do. Getting into a fight with his dad struck him as being bizarre. His dad was such a peaceful person and the last person he could imagine getting into a fight with anybody, let alone his own son. Andy must have felt quite helpless in his situation.

"My mom kept insisting that she had tripped and hit her head, that was why she had a black eye, but I knew that wasn't the truth. It was pretty obvious that Ross, being the kind of guy he is, was the one responsible. Things kind of went downhill after that. I thought Mom might tell him to get lost, but that didn't happen. She just seemed to accept things the way they were and sank deeper into herself after that. She wasn't the same person. I was bowled over with the fact that she ran away with him after the way he had treated her. What was she thinking?"

"Women sometimes get intimidated in that kind of relationship," Mr. Allison said. "And they lose the strength to resist somebody like Ross. They find it easier just to go along with what their partner says rather than resist and perhaps have to endure more physical pain. It's a vicious cycle."

"Mom's a really strong person," Andy said. "At least I thought she was. But with somebody like Ross telling her what to do all the time, it must have been hard."

Andy's house turned out to be a shack with a picket fence that needed painting. The lawn, if you could call it a lawn, had grown out of control and was now just a weed-infested mess. A canoe lay at the side of the house.

"I'm surprised he left that behind," Andy said, pointing at the canoe. "It was his pride and joy."

Mr. Allison pulled up to the gate and everyone got out. "I wonder if it's been rented out," Andy said. "Maybe somebody new lives here now."

As they approached the front door, it opened, and a man stepped out. He was tall, over six feet, and appeared to be about twenty-five years old. He sported a cowboy hat that sat low on his head and obscured most of his face. To Wayne, he looked like he had just competed in a rodeo.

"Can I help you?" he said, sitting down on the step and taking out a package of cigarettes.

Wayne's dad stepped forward. "Are you living in this place now?" he asked.

The man folded his arms. "I'm renting it. Moved in a couple of weeks ago."

"Oh," Wayne's dad said. "Well, we've come to pick up this young man's possessions. He and his mother lived here before you moved in and he left everything he owned behind."

"There's nothing here," the man said, shaking a cigarette out of the package he was holding and lighting it. "I took everything to the dump. There was just a bunch of junk, nothing of any value that I could see."

Andy shook his head. "All my clothes were here and my computer and a whole lot of other stuff including all my books and my bike. Where are they?"

"Didn't see anything like that," the man said. "Somebody must have stolen your things when you were gone. There's been a lot of thievery going on around here lately." He grinned as though Andy's lost property amused him. "Thieves pick up anything that ain't nailed down these days."

"That's our canoe at the side of the house," Andy countered.

"'Fraid not. That canoe belongs to me. Paid good money for it too."

"Mind if I go around and have a closer look at it?" Andy asked.

The man shook his head. "Yeah, I do mind. You're just going to have to take me at my word that it belongs to me." He stood up. "Now if you gentlemen will excuse me, I got work to do. Be sure and close that gate when you leave."

As they turned around, Wayne looked at his dad and he just shrugged. "There's not much we can do, son. I don't think Andy's things are worth fighting over. Sometimes you just have to let things go."

"He stole Andy's stuff. That's pretty obvious. The guy's nothing but a thief himself."

On the way back home, Andy looked a little disappointed that he had lost all of his possessions. "I had a lot of stuff on my computer that I was working on. I wish I could get it back."

"We could report him to the police," Wayne's dad said, "but I doubt if anything would come of it. That cowboy was in the driver's seat and he knew there wasn't much we could do. I'm sorry about your computer."

"Well, I guess I'm not only homeless, but I haven't got a possession to my name. Is this what they call starting from scratch?"

Wayne laughed. "Hey, you're only fifteen. You've got years to accumulate possessions. Heck, you'll probably own a fine house and car by the time you're twenty-five. That gives you ten whole years. Besides, I've got lots of things to share. You're welcome to them."

"Thanks Wayne. That's real nice of you. Trouble is, whatever you give me will have to be awful small. All I've got is the pockets in these pants that I don't even own."

"Well, you're welcome to them. I got lots of pairs of pants. Fact is, I was just thinking about giving some of them away to the Salvation Army."

"Really?" Andy said, grinning over at him and giving him a skeptical look.

"What we need to do right now is figure out what Andy's next move is going to be," Mr. Allison said. "I'm quite sure you don't want to move back into your cardboard box, mortgage or no mortgage. Right Andy?"

"There's lots of room for him in the basement with me. That hide-a-bed probably isn't too comfortable but we've got other beds upstairs that we can bring down."

"That hide-a-bed was the most comfortable bed I've slept on in my life," Andy said. "But I can't just move in with you guys, can I? I mean that's a pretty big move considering you don't even know me. Don't get me wrong, I would love it, but…I wouldn't want to be a burden."

"What do you think, Dad? Can Wayne stay with us? He hasn't got anywhere else to go and we got lots of room for him. Besides, it would be really neat having a…friend stay with me."

"It's just fine with me," Mr. Allison said. "I'll talk to your mother and see what she has to say. There's no way we're going to toss you out when you haven't got anywhere to go."

"That's real nice of you, sir." Andy looked relieved. "I was almost getting used to sleeping under the stars. It's not something I particularly want to get used to though. That cardboard box doesn't offer much comfort or heat."

Mrs. Allison was in the kitchen when they got home whipping up something that they couldn't identify but looked awfully good anyway.

"How did it go?" she wanted to know. "Did you get your things back, Andy?"

"Unfortunately, we ran into a drugstore cowboy with an attitude," Mr. Allison said. "And he wasn't about to let us any nearer the house than the front step. Claims he took Andy's stuff to the dump."

"That's terrible," Wayne's mom said. "Isn't there something we can do?"

Mr. Allison sat down at the table. "Probably not. It would end up being Andy's word against the cowboy's."

"How unfair is that," Mrs. Allison said. "I hope there wasn't anything too valuable."

"Just my computer and some clothes," Andy said. "The computer wasn't all that valuable, but I had a lot of stuff stored in it that I need. Now it's lost forever I guess."

"I've got a tablet and a laptop," Wayne told him. "You can use the tablet if you want."

Andy and Wayne headed downstairs. Wane wanted his parents to have some time alone together to talk about what was going to happen to Andy. Wayne was really hoping that Andy could stay with them at least for a while if not for a long time. It didn't look like his mother and her boyfriend were about to come back after leaving him like that. They could be a thousand miles away by this time and Andy was probably the last thing on their minds.

Wayne started going through his drawers looking for some clothes that he could give to Andy. He had too much stuff anyway and it would be good to clear out some of his drawers.

Andy sat on the hide-a-bed couch looking out the window. "It's really nice of you to let me stay here," he said. "I know your parents haven't decided anything yet, but you've been so generous. How does a buddy thank you?"

"No thanks needed," Wayne told him as a mound of clothes accumulated on the floor in front of him. "But if I know my parents, they'll be glad to let you stay." Wayne looked thoughtful for a moment. "It'll be great having you here. You and I are going to have lots of fun together. We'll be kind of like brothers, don't you think?"

Andy laughed. "Seeing that were both "only- children", and we're both the same size and age – well, I guess somebody up there is looking out for us."

"More like just a giant coincidence," Wayne said. "But considering what you have been through the last few weeks, I think you deserve a break. It's too bad about your stuff though. If I was a little older and a whole lot taller, I would have knocked that cowboy on his butt. What a jerk."

"Yeah, he reminded me of Ross a little bit. Same surly attitude. Maybe we should introduce them. They'd make a good pair."

After supper, Wayne gave Andy the royal tour. Their house was quite large and had four bedrooms upstairs and Wayne's bedroom downstairs. His bedroom was part of the rec room that had a pool table, a ping pong table, a wet bar and a whole lot of other games that could keep a person occupied for hours.

Upstairs, besides the four bedrooms, there was a den, an office and a sewing room that his mom used as well as a large living room containing a fireplace and a dining room. Why they had all this room for only three people Wayne didn't know. He guessed it had something to do with the fact that when he was a kid, his dad lived in a very tiny house with a lot of kids and never had any privacy until he moved out at the age of eighteen.

"You've got an amazing house," Andy said as he sat down at the piano in the living room. He turned to Wayne and asked, "Who plays the piano?"

"I took lessons for a while, but I wasn't very good at it."

When Andy began to play, Wayne was stunned. He sounded as good as any professional he had ever heard.

"Wow! Where did you learn to play like that?"

Andy looked over at Wayne and grinned. "I just picked it up on my own. My parents are both quite musical so I guess I inherited their talent."

Mr. and Mrs. Allison, hearing Andy play, were standing in the doorway looking as amazed as Wayne felt. When Andy had finished playing, they both clapped.

"Very nice," Mrs. Allison said. "I didn't know we had a maestro in our midst."

"I used to play quite a lot before my dad died. When we moved to that house we visited today, Mom had to sell our piano. We needed the money – so I haven't been playing much lately."

"How many songs do you know?" Wayne asked him.

"If I can sing the song, I can play it on the piano."

"You can sing too?"

Andy grinned. "Well, not so well that anybody would pay money to hear me, but I can carry a tune."

"Didn't I tell you he was extraordinary?" Mrs. Allison said. "Now you might believe me when I say I'm a good judge of character."

Wayne wanted to tell her that he already knew that, but she probably wouldn't believe him.

"Can you play Music Box Dancer?" Wayne asked him.

"Oh sure, that's an easy one. I heard it so many times when the ice cream man drove by, it's firmly implanted in my brain."

When he began to play, Wayne's parents started to dance. It was a special moment. Wayne had never seen his parents dancing. He had to admit, they looked kind of…awkward, but it was obvious that they were enjoying themselves. Andy was grinning like he had just won the lottery as he pounded away on the piano.

It looked like Wayne's new friend was fitting right in.

CHAPTER FOUR

AT SCHOOL ON MONDAY, WAYNE learnt more about Andy. When he had appeared the previous Friday, he was still wearing the clothes he wore when he left home and he looked like one of those homeless people on Skid Row. And the air around him was, to put it kindly, not exactly fresh.

Today, he looked like a different person and he acted like a different person. On Friday, he scarcely lifted his head from his desk, but today in History class his hand was in the air whenever the teacher asked a question. It became obvious that Andy was a smart guy. Even our teacher, Miss Evans, was impressed.

"Hey, how come you're so smart?" Wayne asked him as they walked down the steps of the school and headed for home. "You're like a walking encyclopedia."

Andy shrugged. "Smart parents I guess," he said. "Anyway, the questions she asked were pretty simple don't you think?"

"No, they weren't. I couldn't answer any of them and I'm no bonehead. I get a few A's here and there."

They hadn't walked a block when a car pulled up beside them and the driver's window rolled down. A dark-haired woman looked out.

"Mom?" Andy said, walking over to the car. "Where have you been?"

His mother got out of the car and hugged her son. She was a petite woman with expressive dark eyes that still had a vestige of blackness under them compliments of Ross.

"I'm so sorry, Andrew. I didn't want to leave, but Ross insisted. I just didn't have the strength to resist him. Can you understand that?"

"Where is he now?" Andy asked her.

"I don't know," she said. "And I don't care. Where have you stayed while I've been away? I went to the house, but somebody's living there now."

"This is my friend, Wayne. I've been staying at his place for the last few nights."

Andy's mom looked at Wayne and smiled. "I don't know how to thank you," she said. "You're very kind. I hope it wasn't too much of an imposition."

"We love having him," Wayne replied. "And it isn't an imposition at all."

She shook her head and gave Andy another hug. "I've missed you so much. Did you miss your mom at all?"

Andy looked like he was going to break down, but instead he took his mom's hands and stared at her as though he couldn't quite believe what was happening.

"Of course, I missed you. I thought of you all the time. I was worried that Ross might hurt you again."

"I don't think Ross will be hurting anybody anytime soon. He..."

Andy's mom looked at Wayne and smiled. "I don't mean to be rude, but I need to talk to Andrew privately for a few minutes."

"Of course," Wayne said, as they moved away toward the front of her car. He couldn't resist watching them even though he couldn't hear what they were saying. Whatever Andy's mom was revealing seemed to have a visible effect on him as he grabbed her and held her for several seconds as though protecting her from something. Wayne's curiosity was more than piqued.

After several minutes, they came back both looking pale and a little frightened.

"Sorry about that," Andy said.

"No need to apologize," Wayne told him. "I'm sure you and your mom have a lot to talk over without me breathing down your neck."

"Where are you staying?" Andy asked his mom.

"With a friend. She offered me her couch, but I'm hoping to find something in the next few days. I lost my job so I'm going to have to see what I can find. I can't very well rent anything unless I've got a job. Then you can come and live with me again. It's very nice of Wayne to let you stay at his house, but you can't stay there forever."

"He's no trouble," Wayne told her. "We love having him. He can stay as long as he wants."

"Well, that wouldn't be fair to you or your parents. Just as soon as I find another job and get an apartment, I'll let you know. Then you can come and live with me, Andrew."

"By the way, how did you know where to find me?"

His mom gave him an uncertain look. "I phoned Princess Margaret School and they told me you had turned up here. So, I parked in front of the school and hoped maybe you would make an appearance, and sure enough out you came."

As they watched Andy's mom drive away, Wayne wondered what she had told him when they had spoken privately. He had an idea it had something to do with Ross. If Ross was the kind of person Wayne suspected, his mom might have trouble getting rid of him. He was obviously a very scary guy who didn't seem like he would be happy about Andy's mom walking away from him.

"Did your mom tell you where she's staying?" Wayne asked him, as they continued walking toward his house.

He shook his head. "She didn't know her friend's address, but she said she would contact me as soon as she got a job and a place of her own."

Wayne was a little disappointed. Having Andy stay with them was a real treat, not only for him but for his mom and dad, who both liked Andy.

"It must be hard for your mom," Wayne said. "Her life has really been turned upside down. I sure hope she does O.K. Let's hope that our friend Ross doesn't turn up and make her life miserable."

"That's not likely to happen," he told Wayne. "I need to tell you something but you've got to promise to keep it to yourself. That's very important."

They were cutting through a park and sat down on one of the benches that faced a small pond.

"I'm pretty good at keeping secrets," Wayne told him as they turned and faced each other. "Is it about Ross?"

He nodded. "She told me she thinks she killed him. They were staying in a motel and when he passed out after drinking himself into a stupor, she hit him over the head with a heavy stone she found outside the motel. I guess he was bleeding pretty good when she left. He had threatened to kill her if she tried to leave him so I guess that was the final straw as far as she was concerned."

'Holy cow." Wayne could scarcely believe what he was hearing. "She must be in shock over something like that. I can't imagine how she must feel."

"I wonder if she really did kill him," Andy said. "She might have just knocked him out."

"I guess it would depend on how big the rock was and what kind of force she used to drop it on his head." Wayne sighed. "Your poor mom. I wouldn't ordinarily wish someone dead, but it might be better for everybody if Ross never woke up."

As they made their way home, they speculated about what would happen to Andy's mom if indeed she had killed Ross. Would she go to jail for the rest of her life? Perhaps because he had abused her both physically and mentally, the courts would look upon her situation favorably.

Of course, there was also the other fear – that Ross was still alive. That thought was even more scary than the alternative. Ross being what he was, would be out for revenge and Andy's mom's life would be in danger.

"What are you going to do?" Wayne asked Andy. "I think we're going to have to tell my parents. Keeping a secret like that is going to be very hard."

Andy nodded. "I think you're right. They've got a right to know."

"Well, how did things go at school today?" Wayne's mom wanted to know as soon as the boys got in the door. She was sitting in the living room reading a magazine and having a cup of tea. "I hope you didn't get into any fights." She laughed and then seeing the expressions on their faces, stood up and approached them.

"Is everything okay? You two look like you've lost your best friend."

"It's worse than that," Wayne said. He looked over at Andy and he nodded.

"Oh, my gosh, what happened? Come right over here and sit down. I want to hear all about it."

They sat down across from Wayne's mom. They must have looked like two delinquents about to be chastened for skipping class or harassing the teacher, Wayne thought. At that moment, however, Wayne would have chosen either one of those options instead of what really happened.

"We ran into Andy's mom," he said. "She waited outside the school until we came out and then honked at us."

"Well that's good news, isn't it?" Mrs. Allison looked appealingly at Andy. "You weren't exactly expecting her any time soon were you?"

"No, I wasn't and it was really nice to see her."

"Then what?" Mrs. Allison looked confused.

"She…she ah…" Andy looked at Wayne and took a deep breath. It was obvious that he wasn't up to telling Wayne's mom what had transpired.

How did one explain what his mom had told him? It was almost too incredible to believe.

Andy sat with his head in his hands, looking away.

"His mom thinks she might have…killed her boyfriend, Ross," Wayne said.

"What?" Mrs. Allison sat bolt upright, her eyes as round as teacups. "That's awful. How would something like that happen?"

"I think he threatened her," Andy finally said. "It had to be self-defense. There's no other answer. My mom has always been a peace-loving person. She wouldn't hurt a flea. Honest she wouldn't."

"I hardly know what to say. Your poor mom. She must be traumatized having to live with something like that," Mrs. Allison said. "Where is she now?"

"I'm not sure," Andy said. "She didn't say. She just said that she was staying with a friend. I guess I should have got her address, but I was so blown away with what she told me that I didn't even think of it."

Wayne's mom sat looking thoughtful. Finally, she said, "We've got to do something, but I'm not sure what. It looks like you're going to just have to wait until she contacts you again, Andy."

Andy nodded. "The only thing I'm afraid of right now is that…well, what if she didn't kill him? He's likely to come after her. Her life could be in real danger."

"Maybe we should contact the police," Wayne suggested.

"But what could we tell them? We don't even know where Mom is and they might not even do anything anyway. Besides, I don't want to be the one responsible for sending her to jail in case she did kill Ross."

"Did she tell you where all this took place?" Mrs. Allison asked.

Andy shook his head.

"If she did kill him, it would surely be reported in the news, but if we don't hear anything, that could mean Ross is still alive," Wayne said.

Mrs. Allison looked at the boys and sighed. "I'm so sorry all this is happening to you Andy, but I honestly don't think there's much we can do right now – at least not until your mom contacts you again. You boys might as well relax and wait things out. I know that is going to be hard to do, but I don't think there's any alternative."

"The only thing I can suggest," Wayne said, "Is to drive around and see if we can spot your mom's car, but that might be like trying to find a needle in a haystack."

Mrs. Allison got up and went into the kitchen. "You boys need something to eat to take your minds off this. Anybody for pizza?"

Wayne didn't think either one of them was very hungry at that moment, but maybe his mom was right. They probably did need something to distract them.

"Pepperoni for me," Wayne yelled. He looked over at Andy. There was real fear on his face. He didn't envy Andy trying to get through the next few days with the thought that Ross was still alive with murder on his mind.

CHAPTER FIVE

When Mr. Allison got home that night, they told him what had happened. He looked surprised then sat us down and proposed a solution.

"I would say that the first thing we have to do is find your mom," he told us. "Do you have any idea where she might be, Andy?"

Andy shook his head. "I don't. She didn't really have any friends. Ross made sure of that and if she didn't come home right after her shift at the restaurant was over, he was on the phone right away."

"Hmm. Was there anywhere in particular she liked to go? Did she have a favorite spot she enjoyed visiting? Anything like that?"

Andy sat thinking for a few minutes. "Well, she really likes animals and enjoyed going to the zoo. That's the only thing I can think of. Oh yeah, she liked driving around looking at all the million dollar houses with their swimming pools and tennis courts. I guess after living in modest houses all her life, she would like to have lived in something more luxurious."

"Well, that's a start. What kind of a car does she have?"

"It's a silver colored 2008 Toyota. It's really Ross's car, but he made her sell her car. He didn't want her to have any independence so he insisted she sell it. She used his to go back and forth to work. When he wanted to use it, he drove her to work and picked her up after her shift."

"Didn't he work himself?" Wayne's dad asked.

Andy shook his head. "He worked at a planer mill somewhere, on and off, but he would disappear sometimes and then show up a few days later. I don't know what he was doing. Probably selling drugs because he always seemed to have some money when he wasn't bumming some from my mom."

"I think we have to drive around and see if we can spot your mom's car. I know it's a long shot, but it might be worth it. It's pretty hard to hide something as big as a car. We could start at the zoo and work our way over to Cyprus Heights where all the luxury homes are. What do you think?"

"I guess it would be a start," Andy said, looking around at the rest of us. "It's better than sitting around wondering if we're ever going to hear from her again. I sure appreciate you doing this for me, sir."

Mr. Allison looked at his watch. "We can have a late supper. That way we'll have a few hours to look around. What do you say we get started?"

They all piled into Mr. Allison's truck, Andy, Mr. and Mrs. Allison and Wayne and drove over to the zoo. Sunnyside Park sat next to the zoo and was always crowded with people enjoying the trails and walks that it provided. There were lots of spaces for cars but none of them belonged to Andy's mom. After spending almost an hour driving up and down the hills that formed the park, they finally gave up and headed for Cyprus Heights.

They were all amazed at the houses that dominated Cyprus Heights. Some seemed almost a block long with huge lawns and gardens surrounding them. Most of them were set well back from the street and had security gates. You couldn't just drive right into very many of them. It was an eye-opener seeing how the rich lived and the amount of money they spent on their houses. Most people would never make enough money in their lifetimes to buy any of them. No wonder Andy's mom enjoyed looking at them and probably wishing that one day she might live in one.

It took almost an hour to cover the several streets and boulevards that constituted Cyprus Heights but they didn't see any sign of Andy's mom's car. It would have stood out like a blight on the landscape or maybe towed away being in the vicinity of all the limousines, Cadillacs and BMW's that graced most of the homes.

Just as they emerged from Cyprus Heights, they spotted a car that matched Andy's description on a side street under a stand of elm trees. It was almost hidden and if they hadn't been looking in the right direction, they would never have seen it.

As they approached it, Andy's said, "Yeah, that's it. I recognize the logo on the back bumper." It read in large letters: CARPE DIEM: SEIZE THE DAY. IT MIGHT BE YOUR LAST.

As they pulled up beside it, they could see it was occupied. Just about then, Andy's mom's head popped up. She had obviously been lying down in the front seat.

"Mom?" Andy yelled.

She reached over and rolled down the window, looking surprised and a little embarrassed.

"What are you doing here?" she asked.

Andy couldn't help smiling. "Mom, more to the point, what are YOU doing here? I thought you were staying with a friend."

"Oh…yeah, well, she's not home right now, so I've had to stay in my car. But it's only temporary. She should be home tomorrow."

"Are you sleeping in your car?" Andy asked incredulously.

His mom nodded. "I am. But it's just temporary."

Andy got out of the car along with everybody else and approached her window. "This is the Allison family," he told her. "I'm staying with them until you get a place for us."

"I'm Allen," Mr. Allison said, reaching in to shake hands with Andy's mom. She reluctantly took his hand.

"Janet," she said.

"This is my wife, Sandra," Mr. Allison said, as Mrs. Allison reached in also to shake her hand.

"You have a very thoughtful son," Mrs. Allison said. "We've certainly enjoyed having him stay with us. He entertained us with his piano playing yesterday. He's very talented."

"He is," Janet said uncertainly. "He's a very smart boy."

"You are welcome to come and stay at our place until your friend comes home," Mr. Allison offered. "I'm sure it would be much more comfortable and safer than staying in your car."

"I wouldn't want to inconvenience you," Andy's mom said. "Looking after one guest without adding me, is probably more than I dare ask."

"Aren't you afraid staying out here all by yourself?" Andy asked his mom.

"Not really," she said. "The crime rate in places like this is very low. I don't think I've got much to worry about." She turned to Wayne's parents. "I sure do appreciate you looking after Andy. That is very kind of you. I'll try to take him off your hands as soon as I can."

"Aren't you afraid of...Ross?" Andy asked.

His mother gave him a warning look. "Not at all," she finally said. "I don't think Ross will be much of a threat anymore."

"But what if he is," Andy persisted. "He could hurt you badly, maybe even kill you. He's that crazy."

"Your old mom can look after herself," she insisted. "You forget how tough I am. Right?"

"I know how tough Ross is and that worries me," Andy said.

"We sure wish you would come back to our house with us," Sandra Allison said. "We would feel much better about that if you did. And you wouldn't be any inconvenience at all. We would enjoy having your company."

"I can't. I really can't explain it, but I need to be on my own tonight. I need to think things through and plan my next move. I hope you understand."

Mr. Allison shrugged. The sun was about to set and it would be dark in minutes which made things seem even more menacing.

"Could you give us the address of your friend and her phone number so that we can keep in contact with you?" Mr. Allison asked.

Andy's mom shook her head. "I don't know her address or phone number. I'll have to contact you."

Mr. Allison took out his wallet, extracted something from it and handed it to Andy's mom. "Our address and phone number is on that piece of paper. Please call us as soon as you can. We'll be waiting."

As they pulled away, Andy looked out the back window and heaved a sigh. "I hate to leave her there all by herself. I wonder why she won't come with us. She's so…so vulnerable. Anything could happen to her."

'Let's just hope nothing does," Mr. Allison said.

CHAPTER SIX

As Janet Morrison watched the Allison family drive away, she felt suddenly unsure. Had she done the right thing? Was she really in that much danger? There's no doubt, it would be more comfortable in the Allison home. Sleeping in your car was not the most pleasant experience and what if someone came knocking on her window? How scary would that be and how would she cope with it? If it were the police, what would she tell them? Well, she had survived the experience last night even though it hadn't been pleasant. But at least no one had bothered her.

And what about Ross? What if the rock she had dropped on his head hadn't killed him after all? She hadn't taken the time to check whether he was still breathing. All she wanted to do was get out of there and get as far away as she could. She now wished that she had checked to see if he was breathing. She couldn't imagine him living through the trauma of a large rock she could scarcely lift knocking the life out of him.

She stared out the windshield of her car at the pleasant street before her. The sun was just about to set which gave the scene before her a somewhat surrealistic aspect. It looked so peaceful. How was it possible that her life had become so complicated, so impossible amid this beautiful setting? She hated lying to Andy about having a friend's place to go to. The fact was, she didn't have a real friend in the world. Yes, some of the other waitresses were friendly enough but none of them could be considered a real friend. She had never socialized with them outside of the restaurant. Ross would never have tolerated anything like that. As far as Ross was concerned, the only person she need be concerned about was him and him alone. How dispiriting was that? And why had it taken so long for her to recognize what he had done to her?

Well, he was dead now so she no longer had to think about him. And she was a murderer or a murderess as they say. She shuddered at the sound of the word. Had she really killed somebody? It all seemed like some kind of a dream, or nightmare. She hadn't heard anything on the radio about a man being killed by a rock that dropped on him, but maybe that wasn't so surprising with all the murders being committed these days.

She was going to have to spend the rest of her life in prison if they caught up to her and they would eventually catch her, she was certain of that. Could prison life be any worse than living with a man who watched your every move, criticized and complained about almost everything you did? And punched you when he flew off the handle over some trivial thing that bothered him?

Poor Andrew. All this drama around his life. It wasn't fair that he was unable to lead the kind of life every teenager deserves. He was such a great kid and so bright. He could have a wonderful future if only he had the opportunity to make something of himself.

She lay back on the front seat and closed her eyes, but she couldn't sleep. She immediately began to relive dropping the rock on Ross's head. What had possessed her to do that? Why couldn't she have just driven away? After all, Ross was passed out on the bed and wasn't likely to wake up any time soon.

But she knew all too well the answer to that. Ross would come after her with a vengeance and there was no telling what he might do. Her life would never be safe. She would be constantly looking over her shoulder wondering when he was going to make an appearance. The thought made her shudder. Would her life never be normal again?

After ten minutes, she sat up and looked out her windshield. It was dark now and somehow much scarier. She began to wish she had taken up the Allison's offer.

She reached down for her purse, checking to see how much money she had left. There were several twenty dollar bills and some change in her change purse. Not much, but enough for a couple of meals. At least she wouldn't starve. She was hungry now. Maybe that was why she couldn't go to sleep.

She laughed to herself. Compared to the specter of Ross, being a little hungry was incidental.

She sat thinking for several minutes and then decided that maybe something to eat would help, even in a small way. She hadn't had much sleep the previous two nights.

She started her car and pulled away. She remembered a restaurant not far away where she could get a sandwich and something to drink. It would at least take her mind off things for a while and perhaps help her to sleep, although that seemed unlikely.

As she slipped into a booth at The Cozy Cafe, she decided to make inquiries about a waitressing job. Why not? It was a perfectly nice little restaurant and she needed a job desperately. And she was good at it. Everybody told her so.

She ordered a BLT and a cup of coffee and sat looking around. There weren't many customers. The dinner hour had come and gone she guessed, and there was a lull before the nine o'clock crowd began to filter in.

"Do you know if there are any waitressing jobs open?" she asked the young girl who was serving her.

The waitress shrugged. "I don't really know. You could ask Louis. He's the boss, but he's gone for the day. Maybe if you came back tomorrow, you could talk to him."

"Thanks," Janet said. "What time does he come in?"

"Usually about eight. Sometimes a little later. He's a nice guy so if you're any good, he'll probably hire you." She stuck out her hand. "My name's Marjory."

Janet shook her hand. She was much younger than Janet but friendly and if there was anything Janet needed right now, it was a friend.

"How long have you been working here?" Janet asked.

"Only a couple of months. It's a good place to work. Nobody hassling you all the time like in my last job."

Janet finished her meal and headed for the door. "See you tomorrow, Marjory," she waved as she left the restaurant.

After another restless sleep, Janet sat up and looked around. Cars were going by and people were on the move. A few stared over at her as they went by. They were probably wondering what she was doing parked there so early in the morning. Well, she wasn't doing anything illegal so she didn't have to worry about the cops arriving and telling her to move on like some vagrant.

She looked at her watch. It was almost seven o'clock, an hour before Louis would arrive at the restaurant. She could drive around for an hour, but that would be expensive considering there was less than a half-tank of gas left and no money to get a fill-up.

She decided to go for a walk since all she had been doing for the last few days was sitting in her car. She needed to stretch her legs.

She grabbed her purse and stepped out of the car. A perfect blue sky and a light breeze met her and she momentarily felt as though perhaps life wasn't so bad after all.

She walked up and down several streets admiring the well-kept houses and gardens along the way. She had once lived in a house not so different from these, but that had been a long time ago. So much had changed since then and not for the good. Where had things gone so bad? It seemed as though one day her life was pretty normal, she was happy and contented and then everything seemed to go south. Was it something in her makeup that caused her life to be so complicated, so mixed up?

As she turned the corner to return to her car, she could see someone standing beside it. As she drew nearer, her heart almost leaped into her throat. Was it possible? No, it couldn't be. But it certainly looked like him.

She ducked behind a tree and stood observing whoever it was. Surely it couldn't be Ross. Hadn't she dropped a huge rock on his head? Was it possible he had survived? Was the man made out of steel?

She watched for several minutes as he stood smoking a cigarette and looking around. It was Ross all right. Even though she was too far away to make out his features, she could tell by the way he moved that it was him.

My god, what was she to do now? He had obviously recognized his car. But how had he known where to look? She glanced at her watch. It was already twenty to eight. She had to get to that restaurant and talk to Louis, but how would she be able to do that now with Ross standing beside his car?

She noticed another car parked not far away. Obviously, he had either stolen it or borrowed it from somebody, although she couldn't think of anybody who would trust him with their car.

How long was he going to stand there? He couldn't stand there all day, could he? She sighed. Knowing Ross, he definitely could and probably would so she had to do something besides hide behind a tree.

But what?

CHAPTER SEVEN

The Cozy Cafe was a long walk from where she was standing.

There was no alternative but to walk to the restaurant. It was at least a mile or two, but what other choice did she have? She could phone Mr. Allison, but she was reluctant to do that. She didn't want to involve him in her problems. Things were bad enough without the possibility of feeling guilty should things go bad with Ross and that was almost a certainty considering his past.

She began backing up, keeping the trees between her and Ross. When she reached a stone fence, she ducked behind it and then scrambled along until she was out of his sight. She heaved a sigh of relief that he hadn't seen her and began walking as quickly as she could in the direction of the restaurant. Once she had talked to Louis and he hired her, she didn't know what she was going to do. Ross's car was her only defense from the elements.

Perhaps, she thought, if she was hired, she might be able to rent a room somewhere, but without any money that might be difficult. She could also take up the Allison's offer and stay with them until she had earned some money.

Half-an-hour later, Janet spied the restaurant and almost ran the last hundred yards toward it as though Ross was pursuing her. She burst into the restaurant and stood panting at the door as several of the customers turned to stare at her. She took a deep breath and sat down at a booth near the door. Her friend Marjory was nowhere in sight much to her disappointment.

"What can I get you, dear?" another waitress asked. She was a perky matronly-looking woman with a wide smile and dancing blue eyes. Janet suddenly began to relax and smiled back.

"Is Louis in?" she asked.

"Oh, you're the girl looking for a job, right?" When Janet nodded, she added, "Marjory told me about you. I'm Rosalee. She said to treat you like royalty, that you were a real nice girl." She laughed. "I can see that she was right."

"Thank you," Janet said. "That was kind of her."

"I think Louis's in his office." She pointed toward a hallway that led toward the back of the restaurant. "You just go and knock on his door. He'll be glad to see you. Good waitresses are hard to find."

Louis turned out to be a very large man, who probably weighed over 300 pounds. Despite his size, Jane found him to be less than intimidating. There was something almost shy about him as he ushered her into his office.

'I'm Louis," he said as he led her to a chair in front of his desk. After sitting down opposite her and breathing heavily with the effort, he smiled across at her. "Can I get you anything? Tea? A coke? Coffee?"

Janet shook her head. She would have loved a cup of coffee, but wanted to concentrate on getting a job. Once she had that secured, she could then enjoy having something to eat.

"So…what can I do for you, little lady?" he asked, taking a sip of his coffee and peering at her over the rim.

Janet took a deep breath. She still felt winded after walking all the way to the restaurant with the distinct feeling that Ross was right on her heels. Would she never be rid of that man? Well, at least she wasn't a murderer, she thought. And she wouldn't be going to jail, but now she had to keep looking over her shoulder with the fear that he might show up at any moment. Could anything be worse than that?

"I'm a waitress," Janet said. "And I'm looking for a job. I was hoping you might have an opening."

Louis smiled at her. "I always need good waitresses," he said, putting his coffee cup down and leaning toward her. "However, my standards are quite high. I expect a lot from my waitresses. That's why I pay them more than the usual going rate." He paused. "So…are you any good? Do you like waitressing? More to the point, do you like people?"

Janet had never been asked questions like this in her previous jobs. She wasn't quite sure how to answer him. Of course, she liked people, well, most people anyway, and she was a good waitress. She knew that, but how was she to convince Louis?

"You see," he added. "If you like people, then you are probably going to be a good waitress. Does that make sense?"

"It does," Janet said. "It definitely does. And yes, I do like people."

Louis laughed. He had a wonderful laugh that was quite contagious and made her relax. A few minutes ago she was anxious as though Ross was about to burst through the front door of the restaurant and grab her around the neck and drag her out to his car. Now she was beginning to relax, trying her best to forget what had taken place only an hour ago.

"Where did you work last?" Louis finally asked her. "And why did you quit?"

"At the Ambassador," Janet said. "And I quit…because my live-in boyfriend kidnapped me, took me away from my home and left my fifteen-year-old son to fend for himself."

She could hardly believe what she had just uttered. Why was she telling him this? Surely this wasn't something he needed to know. Now he was almost certain not to hire her. If there was one thing a boss didn't need it was an employee who had a whole load of problems.

'I'm sorry to hear that," Louis said. "Have you reported him to the police?"

Janet shook her head.

"An abusive boyfriend huh? I know the kind. My daughter was married to one. I did my best to try to talk some sense into her head, but she was determined to marry the guy. He ended up almost killing her, before she got the courage to leave him, and believe me leaving him was no picnic. The guy wasn't going to let her go without a fight. I finally had to step in and…well, I won't tell you what I did. Let's just say that when I finished with him, he wasn't so keen to get back together with my daughter.

"Anyway, where is your son now?"

"He's staying with some friends until I can get back on my feet."

"Well, I'm quite willing to give you a chance, see how you work out. Where are you staying?"

"I was staying in my car, but that's gone now. It was actually my boyfriend's car, but…" The tears began to run down her face. She hadn't wanted to break down in front of this kind man, but here she was acting like a chastened juvenile caught with her hands in the till.

"I'm so sorry. I didn't mean to involve you in all this, but I really am quite desperate. I need the job so I can find somewhere my son and I can live. I also need to get a car."

"What about this boyfriend? Is he going to be a problem? If he is, maybe I can be of help. Not many guys want to take me on as you can probably see for yourself. I can be quite intimidating when I want to be."

"That's very kind of you," Janet said. "But I can't involve you in this. It wouldn't be right. You hardly know me."

"If you're one of my employees, then I'm automatically involved. Nobody messes with my waitresses. You get me?"

Janet smiled. Where did people like this come from? Why was he being so kind?

"Well, before you can work here, you've got to find yourself a place to live – at least temporarily. Staying in your car is out of the question."

Louis swung away from her and looked out the window. Then he laughed. "I've got the perfect solution," he said, swinging back to face her. "My friend Tony owns a motel not too far from here. You can stay there until you find an apartment. How does that sound?"

"I don't have any money to pay for it," Janet said. "I've scarcely got enough to feed myself for the next day or two."

"Don't worry about paying Tony," Louis said. "He's a friend of mine. I'll talk to him. You can pay him later once you have a little cash in your purse. And when you work here, you eat here, so you're not going to starve. Does that sound okay?"

Janet nodded, hardly able to believe that anyone could be so kind.

"Tony's motel is down the street about three blocks. It's called The Barclay Motel. You can't miss it. A very nice place. You'll like it. Guaranteed."

When Louis came around from his desk, Janet gave him a big hug. "You are a very special person to do this for me. I hardly know what to say except thank you."

"Well, let's just see how things turn out. You can start tomorrow if you like. We've got uniforms here. Charlotte will show you around and let you know the routine. We open at 7 a.m. I don't usually come in until about eight. So, I'll see you then."

"I need something to eat or I'm going to faint," Janet said, heading for the door. "Thanks again, Louis, and I'll see you in the morning."

After having a solid breakfast of bacon and eggs, toast and coffee, Janet headed out the door to find the Barclay Motel. The thought of being able to sleep inside on a proper bed with blankets and a TV to watch seemed like a dream come true. What was even better was the fact that Ross would have no idea where she was, so she didn't have to worry about him showing up on her doorstep. And staying only three blocks from the restaurant meant that she didn't need a car, at least not at the present moment.

The Barclay Motel was a red and white structure set well back from the road. It looked as though it had been built within the last few years, very ornate like it was right out of Disneyland. Janet sighed with relief when she finally arrived at the office door.

Tony was an elderly man with a grizzled beard and friendly blue eyes. "You must be Janet," he said, when Janet presented herself at the counter. "Louis just phoned and told me you need a place to stay. And I've got the perfect room for you. It looks right out onto the lake at the back where nobody can bother you. Does that sound okay?"

"It sounds wonderful," Janet said.

"Follow me then and I'll show you the room. If you don't like it, don't worry, I've got lots of other rooms."

"I'm sure I'll like it." Janet had to smile to herself considering the conditions under which she had existed for the last few nights. The room, whatever it turned out to be, had to be infinitely better than her car.

The room turned out to be perfect. It was clean and comfortable and had a king size bed. She had never slept on a bed that big in her life. And Tony was right. It had a beautiful view out the back window and it did afford her the privacy that she craved at that moment.

Janet fell backwards onto the bed and was almost instantly asleep.

CHAPTER EIGHT

HE WAS FURIOUS. THAT STUPID WOMAN HAD DROPPED A rock on his head and broken several teeth and left him with a headache to end all headaches. He felt as though he was falling into a deep pit whose depth never seemed to end.

After several agonizing minutes, Ross was able to gain his feet, but he was so wobbly, he could scarcely stand up straight. It wasn't bad enough that he had way too much to drink, but having a rock dropped on his head, made the world seem like something out of a recurring nightmare. The room he was in kept spinning until he finally had to sit down on the bed again to gain control of himself. His mouth was bleeding and he had spit out several teeth.

"I'm going to kill her," he said to himself. "And very slowly. She's going to regret the day she met me."

Ten minutes later, and not feeling much better than he had when he regained consciousness, he left the motel room only to find that his car was missing.

"That bitch! I'm going to…"

"Hey," somebody yelled at him. "You checking out?"

Ross looked around. Some old guy was staring at him from the door of the office. He glanced at his watch. It was almost three o'clock in the afternoon. Where in hell had all the time gone?

"Yeah, yeah. Somebody stole my car."

"That was your wife," the old guy said. "She barreled out of here like the devil himself was after her. You two have a fight?"

Ross wouldn't have considered what went on between him and Janet a fight exactly. More like an attempt at murder. He should be calling the cops instead of… Well, guess calling the cops wouldn't be a wise option, he thought. The silly bitch would probably accuse him of kidnapping her or something. Considering she was his common-law wife, it didn't seem very logical that any court would find him guilty of kidnapping. Wasn't a wife supposed to do her husband's bidding, go where her husband wanted her to go? Do what he told her to do without a lot of whining and carrying on?

"Just a little misunderstanding," Ross told the old guy. Now he recognized the man as the one who had checked them in the night before. Was he going to charge him for an extra day just because he was leaving a few hours late? That didn't seem very logical considering that most of the motel rooms were empty anyway.

"Did you see what direction my wife went when she left?"

"I wouldn't tell you even if I knew," the old man said. "You scared the dickens out of her."

"She scares easy," Ross said. "She's real skittish."

The old man shook his head. "It looked to me like she had reason to be skittish. You ain't one of them abusive types, are you?"

"Could you call me a taxi?" Ross asked him. He wanted to tell the old guy to mind his own business, but there was no sense in getting on his bad side, especially since he needed to get into town as soon as he could and needed a taxi to do that.

"I'll do it," the old man said, shaking his head. "But only because your wife seemed like a real nice lady. I hate to see guys like you mistreating women. It's not right."

She tried to kill me, Ross wanted to yell at him as he watched the old man return to the office to phone for a taxi. Wasn't he the one being mistreated? His mouth was so sore, he could hardly talk, let alone think. Seeing a dentist was out of the question right now, even if he could afford it. He was just going to have to walk around looking like a prize fighter who had taken a few too many punches. But it was nothing like Janet was going to look like once he got his hands on her.

"Somebody'll be along in a couple of minutes," the old guy said, leaning out the door of the office. "Don't come back."

A taxi drew up ten minutes later.

"Do you know where I can rent a car?" Ross asked the taxi driver. "My wife drove off with mine."

"Sure thing," the taxi driver said.

He dropped Ross off in front of a Hertz rent-a-car. Ross took out his wallet to pay the cabbie and was shocked at the small amount of cash he had. He was going to have to either rob a bank or take out a loan, neither of which was an option, unfortunately. He handed the cabbie the fare, minus a tip, and grinned when the cabbie glared at him. There were times, he decided, when a tip just wasn't practical.

Ten minutes later, Ross drove away in a shiny new Chevrolet, having paid for it with his credit card that was about to be maxed out.

Now it was time to find Janet. The most logical place to look for her was back at their house. But that was several hundred miles away. It was going to take some driving and in his condion it wouldn't be easy. But finding her was his main priority. Nothing was going to stop him from getting his hands on her.

Maybe their house hadn't been rented out yet, and besides, he wanted to see if his canoe was still there. On second thought, it didn't seem likely that Janet would return to their former home, if you could call it a home, because she would know that would be the first place he would look for her.

Well, he had to start somewhere.

When he knocked, the door was opened by a tall, well-built dude wearing a cowboy hat. It looked as though his landlord hadn't lost any time renting the place out after he had left.

"Name's Ross. I used to live here." He held out hand but the cowboy didn't take it.

"What do you want?" the cowboy asked.

"I left my canoe here and a bunch of other stuff," Ross said. "Guess you wouldn't mind if I pick them up."

"I guess I would mind. That canoe is mine and there's nothing else. I took a whole bunch of stuff to the dump. None of it looked like it was worth bothering about. Just a lot of junk."

Ross folded his arms and glared at the cowboy. "That canoe is worth a lot of money and I mean to have it. I'll have to come back later with a truck. You're not going to give me a lot of hassle about it, are you?"

The cowboy laughed. "Your chances of walking away with that canoe are less than zero, fella. I own it and I aim to keep it, so let's not get too excited." He peered closely at Ross. "You don't look so good with all those teeth missing. What did you do, run into a steam roller?"

"I can prove its mine," Ross said.

"Don't matter. Possession's nine-tenths of the law. Didn't they teach you anything at school?"

"It's got my name on the inside up toward the front. I guess that ought to convince you it's mine."

"Don't know your name, don't know you from Adam and furthermore don't want to know you. If I were you, I'd just head right out of here while you still got some teeth left."

"Is that a threat?" Ross said.

"Sure sounds like one to me," the cowboy said.

When Ross started moving toward the canoe, the cowboy came down off the steps and moved in front of him. "I'm warning you, fella, just turn yourself around and head out of here right now. I'm about to lose my patience."

"Is that right? Well, I paid good money for that canoe and I mean to have it, so it might be in your best interest to get out of my way so I can show you where my name is."

The cowboy pushed Ross. "Like I said, I don't know your name. You could be anybody. There's already been a bunch here claiming it was theirs."

Ross attempted to push back, but the cowboy grabbed his wrist and twisted hard. Ross yelped with pain as the cowboy pinned his arm behind his back.

"I could break your arm right now," he said. "Is that old canoe worth a broken arm?"

Ross struggled but couldn't free himself from the solid grip the cowboy had on him. "You better let me go," he screamed. "I'll have the cops after you for theft and bodily harm."

The cowboy laughed. "You know what? You don't look like the type who would call the cops. Probably because they're already on the lookout for you. What are you, a drug dealer?" He gave Ross a violent push that sent Ross flying, ending up on the grass looking up at the cowboy.

"Now git, before I really get mad and start breaking some bones."

Ross picked himself up and headed for his car. Before getting there, he turned toward the cowboy. "I'll be back with the cops. When they see all these teeth missing, I'm pretty sure they'll be interested in charging you with assault and battery."

The cowboy grinned, shaking his head. "Somehow, I don't think that's going to happen, pal. But if you don't hightail it out of here right now, I might call them myself and have them arrest you for trespassing."

Ross limped over to his car and sat looking back at the cowboy, who stood with his arms folded, a broad grin on his face. "I sure aim to enjoy that canoe," he yelled. "Always wanted one just like that. It's a real beauty. Bet it cost a pretty penny too."

Ross started the car and drove away, giving the cowboy the finger.

"If I ever see that guy again, I'm going to kill him. I could have taken him if I wasn't so banged up." But Ross knew that wasn't true. That cowboy was tough and strong as an ox. There was no way he was going to tangle with the guy again.

He drove into town and parked outside a restaurant called The Coffee House. It took him several minutes to recover from the indignity of being manhandled by the cowboy. He wasn't used to being pushed around by anybody. He was usually the one doing the pushing.

Finally, he got out of his car and entered the restaurant. He was hungry, not having eaten since the day before. Besides, he needed to relax and figure out his next move. Janet was somewhere in town and the most logical place for her would be a restaurant. He knew that if he began asking around about her, he would eventually find her waitressing somewhere in this town. It was the only thing she knew how to do and he knew she was broke and needed money.

And when he found her…

CHAPTER NINE

"It must have been awful sleeping outside like that," Wayne said to Andy as they sat in the living room of Wayne's house. "Weren't you afraid somebody might come along and rob you?"

"Well they wouldn't have got much if that was their intent," Andy replied. "Because I didn't have much more than the clothes on my back. Anyway, who would be prowling around here at two o'clock in the morning except a guy from my class at school who couldn't sleep?"

Wayne laughed. "You got a point there all right."

"I'm sure glad you couldn't sleep though," he added. "Otherwise I would still be sleeping inside that old box."

"Well, you're sure welcome to stay here as long as you want."

"I'm worried about my mom. I sure wish she would phone. I'm not so convinced that the rock she dropped on Ross's head did the job. And if it didn't, he's going to want to get revenge and I hate to even think about what that might be."

"He sounds like a nasty character," Wayne said.

"Well, he did have a good side when everything was going well, but once things didn't go as he wanted, he got real nasty. It was hard not to be able to do anything when he got abusive with Mom. I sure wanted to plant a fist in his face, but I might have paid a high price for that. He could get violent when provoked and Mom knew that. I guess that's why she always went along with what he wanted instead of standing up for herself. And she was always afraid of what he might do to me. She was very protective of me and didn't want to see me hurt."

"I wonder what we should do?" Wayne said. "It's hard just sitting here waiting for the phone to ring. I feel a little guilty being here when Mom and Dad are out there looking for your mom."

"I wish I had my phone, but unfortunately, I left it back at the house. No doubt our cowboy friend has now taken possession of it. Either that or it's buried beneath a bunch of garbage."

After driving around for several hours looking for Janet's car and not having any success, Mr. Allison said to his wife: "Let's stop at a restaurant and have something to eat. I'm hungry and I think we deserve a break. Besides, Andy's mom was a waitress, wasn't she? Maybe we'll get lucky and she'll end up waiting on us."

Sandra laughed. "I think the chances of that happening are pretty slim wouldn't you say?"

"I think so, but stranger things have happened."

They pulled into a small family restaurant, parked their car at the rear as there were very few parking spots, and entered.

The young lady who served them was definitely not Andy's mother. She was probably thirty years older and forty pounds heavier, but she had a nice smile and looked as though she had been working as a waitress for a long time.

Allen and Sandra ordered a tuna sandwich and a glass of milk. When their order came, they held up their glasses and made a toast. "To peace and contentment in our lives and especially in Andy's life."

They had no sooner clicked glasses when the door opened and a man shouted, "Anybody here own a red Ford half-ton?"

Allen looked at his wife and then over at the man at the door. "We do," he said. "Is something wrong?"

The man came over to their table. "Some kid got into your car and took off with a black bag of some sort. I was parked right next to you and saw the whole thing.

I chased him for about a half-block, but I'm not in such good shape these days."

Allen had to agree with him. He looked like he had had a tangle with a pile driver.

"I'd better go out and check and make sure the truck is okay," Allen said. "I must have forgotten to lock it."

"It's fine," the man said. "He didn't do any damage, and he only got away with the bag, so unless it was full of diamonds, maybe you don't have to worry until after you've eaten."

"That kid is going to be awfully disappointed," Allen said. "That was my gym strip in the bag."

Allen stood up and offered his hand. "I thank you for what you were able to do. That was a nice gesture. Can we buy you a drink?"

"Well, thank you. That's very nice," he said, sitting down beside Sharon. "I could sure do with a beer."

After ordering a beer, Allen looked over at his companion. "I'm Allen Allison and this is my wife Sandra."

"Joe...Joe Smith," the man said, doing his best to smile but not having much success.

"So, what do you do for a living, Joe?" Allen asked.

"Oh, this and that. Right now, I'm looking for my wife. She ran off and took my car. I'm driving a rental right now. I'm anxious to get ahold of her. She's a waitress so I thought maybe she would be working here, but I don't see her. Sure never know what these women will do. Been with her for over two years, helped raise her no-good son and this is the way she repays me."

Allen looked over at his wife who looked like she had seen a ghost. Was it possible this was the notorious Ross?

"So, what does your wife look like?" Allen asked. "Just in case I should see somebody who might be her." He was having a hard time trying to keep a straight face and didn't dare look at Sandra, who must be feeling panicky by this time.

"She's kind of skinny and not very tall, dark brown hair, thirty-eight years old. Looks a bit like a hooker when she's all made up. I got a few issues with her. When I find her, she's not going to be one happy camper I'll tell you that."

"What do you mean by that?" Allen asked.

The man who called himself Joe Smith laughed. "I'll just say that I don't take too kindly to somebody running out on me and stealing my car. So, I've got some settling to do. I'll leave the rest to your imagination."

"I hope you don't mean that you intend to abuse her?"

"Joe laughed again. "Well, she abused me, stole my car. I guess it wouldn't be out of order for me to return the favour."

"Please don't do anything violent," Sandra said. "The poor woman was probably desperate. Beating her up won't solve anything."

Joe finished his beer and stood up. "Thanks for the beer. I gotta roll. Sure nice meeting you folks." With that, Joe Smith walked out of the restaurant.

Allen and Sandra looked at one another and shook their heads. They had completely lost their appetite and soon followed Joe out of the restaurant.

CHAPTER TEN

WHEN JANET WOKE UP, IT WAS DARK AND FOR SEVERAL seconds she didn't know where she was which caused her to panic until she finally realized that she was safe inside her motel room. The thought that Ross was out there somewhere looking for her, anxious to get revenge for having a rock dropped on his head, gave Janet pause.

She switched on a light and glanced at the clock beside her bed. It was almost six a.m. She was supposed to be at work by seven. She felt grubby having slept in her clothes that were badly in need of washing. If she hadn't been so tired the night before, she would have washed her clothes in the sink, but it was too late now. They would never dry by the time she was ready to leave.

She also needed a shower badly, but taking a shower and then climbing back into her smelly clothes was something she didn't want to do. She was glad that they had uniforms at the restaurant. At least she would look somewhat decent once she put on a uniform. She had time to wash her hair at least. It was important that she look her best when she showed up at the restaurant. Louis was a nice guy, but she didn't want to give him any reasons to regret his decision to hire her.

An hour later, Janet left the motel and began to walk the three blocks to the restaurant. It was a mild, sunny day with fleecy white clouds dotting the sky and Janet suddenly felt happier than she could remember. Always having to be on her guard when Ross was around, took the joy out of her life. How had she endured his abuse these last few years? Well, hopefully that part of her life was over. She and Andrew could start rebuilding their lives without Ross's interference. It was going to be difficult avoiding him, keeping out of his sight, but with Louis on her side as well as the Allison's, Ross was going to have more than a little trouble hassling her.

She took a deep breath and looked around. Ross could be following her right this minute, she thought. God, would she never be rid of him. Even if he never found her, she would still be looking over her shoulder, worrying that he was about to pop out in front of her with a knife in his hand. So much for being rid of Ross.

There were several customers waiting to get into the restaurant when Janet arrived shortly before seven. It must be a popular place, she thought. Not even open yet and they were lining up to get in. Maybe that said something about Louis. He was a nice guy and the customers probably appreciated that.

She banged on the window to get one of the waitress's attention. One of them came to the door and opened it. She smiled at Janet.

"Hi, I'm Charlotte and I'll bet you are Janet. Come on in."

"Welcome to the Cozy Cafe," Charlotte said, once Janet was inside. "Have you had any breakfast yet?" When Janet shook her head, Charlotte said, "Well, you just go and get your uniform on and I'll bring you in something to eat. You can't work on an empty stomach."

"Thank you," Janet said, following Charlotte to a closet where the uniforms were hung.

"Hmm. You look like a petite," Charlotte said and presented Janet with a uniform. "Try this one on. It looks about right."

Janet was shown into the staff room where she quickly changed into a uniform and immediately felt more relaxed. It was a relief to shed her dirty clothes after wearing them for several days.

A few minutes later, Charlotte arrived with a breakfast for Janet. "I sure hope you like eggs and hot cakes," Charlotte said.

"I love them," Janet said.

"How about a coffee?"

"Next to eggs and hot cakes, I love coffee. Black please."

Janet's first day at the restaurant was a roaring success. She had always enjoyed socializing with the customers and often traded good-natured barbs with them. The only downside was the fact that every time somebody came into the restaurant, Janet looked over her shoulder, afraid that it might be Ross. The fact that Louis was in his office and had promised to make short work of Ross if he showed up, was somewhat comforting, but she still dreaded the thought of having to confront him.

"You did just fine," Louis told her at the end of the day. "I had a pretty good idea that you would be good at your job and I was right. Now you go home and relax and if that husband of yours shows up, you just give me a call. Here's my cell number. Day or night – it doesn't matter. I'm not going to have some guy messing with one of my girls. Ya hear?"

Janet couldn't help smiling at Louis's sincerity. "I hear you," she told him. "I don't know how to thank you."

"No thanks needed," he said. "You're one fine waitress and that's all the thanks I need."

As she walked back to the motel, Janet suddenly felt an anxiety she hadn't felt all day. What would she do if Ross suddenly made an appearance? There was no doubt he had murder on his mind considering what she had done to him. Now that she had a job and Andrew was no longer homeless, she felt as though the possibility of getting her life straightened around was a distinct possibility.

But she still couldn't resist looking over her shoulder with the fear that Ross might suddenly be right behind her, ready to do her harm.

CHAPTER ELEVEN

As Allen Allison pulled out of the parking lot of the restaurant, he heaved a sigh of relief. Whoever had got into his truck, at least hadn't done any damage and the loss of his gym strip was of little consequence. He just couldn't get over the guy that called himself Joe Smith. There was no doubt in Allen's mind that Joe Smith was Ross.

"Now wasn't that something," Sandra said. "I can understand why Janet is afraid of that man. He's very scary. It seems so out of character for him to tell us about somebody taking something from our car though. And he appeared to be such a nice man…at first, but it didn't take long to discover that Joe Smith alias Ross whatever, was not the fine upstanding person he was portraying."

Allen shook his head. "I'm not sure what we should do now. Well, we at least know what he looks like. But it's not as though we can call the police on him. He hasn't really done anything and he is Janet's live-in husband. I guess Janet could get a restraining order if he's stalking her, but you would have to prove that, wouldn't you?"

"I shudder to think what that man would do to Janet if he caught her alone. That poor woman. If we only knew where she was, we could warn her about him, not that that would do much good. But at least she would be aware that he's looking for her and could be on her guard."

"Somehow, I think she's probably already on her guard."

When they arrived home, Andy had a broad grin on his face. "Mom phoned," he said. "And she's got a job at a restaurant."

"Now isn't that good news," Sandra said. "I'm so happy for her. What's the name of the restaurant?"

"The Cozy Café," Andy said. "And she's staying at a motel not far away. Isn't that great?"

"We've got some news of our own," Mr. Allison said. "We dropped in for a sandwich at a restaurant and you'll never guess who showed up there."

"Ross?" When Mr. Allison nodded, Andy rolled his eyes. "I can't believe it. How did you know it was him?"

"We bought him a beer after he so kindly chased a kid who had got into our car. Once he answered a few of our questions, we were convinced that this had to be Ross. That and the fact that he was missing a few teeth. He's one nasty character I'll tell you. It was nice of him to let us know about the theft from our car, but our impressions of him soon changed."

"That sounds like Ross all right. He can be quite charming when he wants to be. He sure had my mom fooled."

"The question now is, what do we do about him? Your mom isn't safe with him floating around just waiting to catch her unawares," Mrs. Allison said.

"We can't go to the police because he hasn't done anything yet," Wayne said. "That makes things a little awkward. If we wait until he does something, it could be fatal."

"When are you going to be seeing your mom?" Mr. Allison asked.

"Tomorrow after class," Andy said. "The restaurant she's working at is only about a mile from our school. She really seems to like her job there and she likes the owner."

"There's no doubt that Ross will eventually run her down. He's obviously checking out all the restaurants in town," Mr. Allison said. "That might take him a little while but eventually, he's going to find her. Then what?"

Nobody seemed to have an answer.

"I wish she would come and stay with us," Mrs. Allison finally said. "I would feel much better about the whole thing if she was here. She needs people around her to protect her. If she's by herself in a motel, she won't have much protection."

"Mom's pretty independent," Andy said. "She seems determined to find a place for us now that she's got a job."

"Too bad we couldn't hire a…" Wayne chuckled. "I was going to say someone with some clout. You know, somebody six foot six and weighing 250 pounds who could intimidate Ross, make him go away."

"How about the Equalizer?" Mr. Allison asked.

"The what?"

"The Equalizer. It was a TV program featuring a guy who put an ad in the paper saying he would help anybody who was in a situation like your mom is facing – and free of charge. He was very good at putting pressure on stalkers, abusers and the like. It was a great program. I used to watch reruns. Never missed an episode if I could help it. Entirely fiction of course, but it brought up some interesting situations."

"Too bad it was fiction. We could use somebody like that," Wayne said.

"Well, I guess we're just going to have to wait and see what develops," Mr. Allison said. He looked at his watch. "It's getting late and you guys got school tomorrow. Guess we'll have to call it a night."

After Ross left the restaurant, he was beginning to feel a frustration that began in his gut and moved up into his head, giving him a pain that was even more severe than the pain in his mouth where Janet had dropped the rock.

He felt as though he was about to explode if he didn't find her soon. Surely there weren't that many restaurants in this town that he couldn't discover which one she might choose to work in. And he was quite certain that was exactly what she would do. She had never done anything other than waitressing. He knew she didn't have any money so she had to find a job somewhere. But where?

As he sat in his car, he thought about the people who had bought him a beer. They seemed a little strange to him, a little too concerned about what he intended to do to Janet when he caught her. Was it possible they might know her? It seemed like a long shot, but it wasn't out of the question. And his instincts had always served him well. Something told him that maybe, just maybe, those people weren't exactly what they appeared to be.

He pulled out of his parking spot and found another spot close to the entrance of the restaurant. Maybe if he followed them, he might find out just who they were and whether they had anything to do with Janet. He was tired of visiting one restaurant after another with no results. Maybe a change of tactics would pay dividends.

It was easy keeping the red truck in sight as Ross followed the Allison's, keeping well back so that they weren't able to catch sight of him and possibly identify him as the person they had been talking to in the restaurant.

After driving for about fifteen minutes, the Allison's turned off the highway and entered a suburban area replete with trees, shrubs and middle-class homes that reminded Ross of where he had been brought up. When they pulled into a driveway, Ross drove past and circled the block, returning a few minutes later and parking his car half-a-block down the street. It was beginning to get dark and for what Ross intended to do, he would need the cover of darkness to pull it off without being seen.

As he sat smoking a cigarette and looking at the Allison house, which he noted was somewhat grander than most of the houses around it, he sighed. He might well be on a wild goose chase. But his instincts had served him well in the past. And until he was convinced that these people had nothing to do with Janet, he intended to proceed.

He sat thinking of Janet and what he intended to do to her when he got her in his sights. Taking advantage of him while he was asleep and completely at her mercy, struck him as being ample reason for him to chase her down and teach her a lesson she wouldn't soon forget.

After smoking several cigarettes and satisfied that it was now dark enough to proceed, Ross got out of his car and walked toward the Allison house, keeping the trees between him and the windows that looked out onto the street.

He could see a light come on in the basement and immediately moved toward it, thinking that perhaps these people had rented a downstairs room to Janet.

As he approached the basement window, he could see two teen-agers sitting on a couch watching TV, and as he got closer, he almost let out a cry of joy when he identified Andrew as one of the teen-agers.

So, his instincts had been right. Janet, he surmised, was probably upstairs with the owners. He grinned to himself. This was going to be easier than he had thought. Much easier. Little did Janet realize just how big a mistake she had made in crossing him and what he was capable of doing to her to exact his revenge.

CHAPTER TWELVE

THE NEXT MORNING WHEN JANET ENTERED THE RESTAUrant after having slept soundly the night before, Louis was there before her and gestured for her to join him in his office.

"So, how are things going for you so far?" he asked.

"Wonderful," Janet said. "I'm really enjoying the job and the staff has been very helpful."

"I'm pleased with your work, Janet. Charlotte tells me you're one of the best waitresses she's worked with and Charlotte should know. She's been around the block a few times."

"She's been very helpful," Janet said.

Louis leaned back in his chair and smiled at Janet. "How are things at the motel. Are you comfortable there?"

"It's very nice and your friend had been most accommodating. But I'll have to start looking for a permanent place to live. I can't keep living at the motel. I want my son to join me. He's living with another family right now until I find a place."

"Yes, I understand. Any ideas where you would like to live?"

"Somewhere close to the restaurant so I can walk to work. I don't have a car."

"What about your boyfriend? Any sign of him?"

"Thank goodness, no. And if I never see him again, I will be very happy."

"Don't forget my promise. If this guy starts harassing you, all you have to do is let me know, and I'll take care of it."

"You're very kind, Louis. But Ross is one nasty person and unlikely to give up looking for me. This town isn't big enough to hide me for long. I'm afraid he's going to show up one of these days when I least expect it. Not a pleasant thought."

"I'm sorry you have to be put through all this worry. The sooner we can deal with our friend Ross and get him straightened around, the better. In the meantime, I hope you'll be all right and not worry too much about him. You've got friends and we're ready to help you whenever the need arises."

Janet felt somewhat better as she entered the restaurant prepared to begin her shift. Louis was the most considerate boss she had ever worked for, but she wondered if even he could do very much to help her. She knew how determined Ross was to find her and knowing him, he would stop at nothing to repay her for what she had done to him.

After sleeping in his rental car to save money, Ross returned to the Allison's house and waited down the block for the teen-agers to make an appearance. They had to go to school, didn't they? There was a school not far away. Perhaps that was the one they attended.

He glanced at his watch. It was almost eight o'clock. At ten after the hour, a red truck backed out of the garage and drove past him. He could see that it was the man who had bought him a beer the night before.

At eight-thirty the two boys appeared and walked down the street toward him. Ross slumped down in his seat so that he wouldn't be seen as the boys passed him on the other side of the street and continued along the sidewalk in the direction of the school.

When they were a block away, he started his car, did a U-turn and began following them. He wondered where Janet might be. Was she in the same house that the boys had come out of or was she holed up somewhere else? He was hoping that Andrew was going to lead him to her wherever she might be. The first thing he wanted to establish was whether the two boys were attending the high school that was less than a mile away. Once that was established, he would wait for them to make an appearance after school. Perhaps then, Andrew might lead him to where Janet worked, if she had gotten herself a job. If the boys simply returned to the house, then it would be pretty clear that Janet was probably living there as well.

During the day, Ross kept thinking about his canoe, resenting the fact that the cowboy had got the best of him when he had made an attempt to retrieve it. Well, that cowboy was in for a big surprise. Ross had every intention of getting his canoe back one way or another. Having somebody steal his canoe that he had paid good money for did not sit well with him and next to finding Janet, getting the canoe back was high on his priority list. Besides, he was running short on money and since the canoe was practically brand new, he could probably get a fair price for it.

He needed a truck though. There was no way he could fit the canoe in his car. His car wasn't big enough. Not having much money presented a problem, but maybe he could trade his car in on one and make payments. It was always handy to have a truck and it didn't need to be anything fancy. And he could return the rental car and save himself some money on returning it early.

He spent the morning visiting used car lots and finally found the truck that suited both his pocket book and his needs. After talking to the salesman and explaining that he had a car but needed a truck, could he use his car as a down payment on the truck? The salesman wanted to see Ross's car before committing himself to the sale since Ross wasn't employed and had no fixed address.

After dropping off the rental car and setting off to pick up his car that was parked several miles away, Ross drove it back to the used car lot and within ten minutes, the salesman agreed to a sale.

The truck was a half-ton Chevy that had a lot of miles on it, but it appeared to be in reasonable condition. It had a flatbed that was long enough to accommodate a canoe and that was all that Ross was concerned about.

His next concern was how was he going to be able to get the canoe off the cowboy's property and onto the back of his truck? He was going to need some help – but he didn't know anybody well enough to ask them to give him a hand. He was going to have to hire somebody. But who?

As he sat in a café on Main Street and observed the people walking by, he noticed a young man sitting on a bench, idling the time away, smoking one cigarette after another and seemingly having no sense of purpose. He seemed to Ross, a good prospect to help him carry the canoe. Not that he could pay him much. Ross was down to his last fifty dollars with no idea what he might do once he was out of money. That made retrieving his canoe all the more urgent. But first things first.

He left the café and approached the young man, who appeared to be in his late teens.

He sat down beside him, took out a packet of cigarettes and offered the young man one. He eagerly took it and leaned over while Ross lit it for him.

"Like to make twenty dollars?" Ross asked him. "Ten minute's work. Easy money."

"Sure. What do I have to do? Kill a snake."

Ross laughed. "Nothing quite that dangerous. Help me carry a canoe and load it on my truck."

"For twenty bucks? Hardly worth my time."

"Okay, thirty bucks then."

The young man appeared to be considering the offer. Finally, he grinned. "How about forty? I could probably do it for forty."

Ross could hardly believe this kid. Who did this lay about think he was anyway to demand forty dollars? Of all the nerve. "All right. You drive a hard bargain, kid."

"I didn't get to be where I am now by being a lemon." He grinned over at Ross and winked. "So, when is this job to take place?"

"Tonight. At midnight. I'll meet you right here."

"Midnight? What are you planning to do? Steal the canoe?"

"Just getting back what belongs to me. He stole it from me so I'm stealing it back."

"Don't know if I want to get involved in something like that," the kid said. "I'm already in the cops' bad books. I'll need at least fifty since it involves theft. And I'll need twenty-five up front."

Ross wanted to grab the kid around the neck and give him a good shaking and that was exactly what he would have done if he didn't need him so badly. Well, he could give the kid twenty-five bucks and refuse to pay him the rest after the job was done. What could he do? Call the cops?

He took out his wallet and gave the kid twenty-five dollars. "Don't be late. I'm anxious to get this job over with. The sooner it's done, the better. Okay?"

"OK," the kid said. "See you at midnight."

As Ross walked away, he shook his head. The kid probably wouldn't show. He's got twenty-five dollars in his pocket for nothing. What a sap he had been. What made him think he could trust this kid? The guy had probably never done a day's work in his life.

CHAPTER THIRTEEN

Ross was surprised to see the kid sitting on the bench in front of the restaurant just like he said he would be. Wonders never cease, he thought. Even though he disliked the kid with a kind of visceral intensity, he was glad to see him.

The kid climbed into the cab of the truck and Ross sped down the road toward his old house. "This shouldn't take too long," he said. "In and out and probably the easiest fifty dollars you'll ever earn."

"Let's hope so," the kid said. "I don't like working in the dark and if anybody shows up, I'm out of there."

As they pulled up to the house, there was just enough light for Ross to see right away that the canoe was no longer sitting where it had been the day before.

"Damn, it's not there," he said.

"So, what do we do now?" the kid asked.

Ross sat looking at the house he had lived in for almost two years and then remembered the shed at the rear of the property, a shed that he had scarcely ever entered. He reached into the glove compartment and took out a flashlight.

"I'll bet he put it in the shed," he said. "Let's go."

They made their way across the lawn and along the side of the house to the rear. When they reached the shed, Ross swore again. There was a lock on the door. After giving the lock a couple of good pulls and realizing it was going to take more leverage than he was able to produce, he turned to the kid. "Maybe there's a way of getting in at the rear. You stay here."

"I'm not staying here by myself," the kid said. "I'm sticking right beside you."

Ross shook his head in disgust. How had he been so lucky to find a helper with the courage of a snail?

"Okay, okay, but don't make any noise. I don't want that cowboy suddenly showing up and..."

"Cowboy? You didn't say anything about a cowboy."

"He lives here now. And he thinks he's going to keep my canoe. But I've got news for him."

"A cowboy," the kid said to himself. "That's all I need now. The price of my assistance is going up by the minute."

"A drugstore cowboy. He probably hasn't been on a horse in his life."

As they rounded the corner of the house and headed for the rear of the shed, Ross could see that the cowboy had fashioned a corral that contained two horses. One of them lifted his head and looked at Ross and Ross could have sworn that the nag winked at him.

"Never been on a horse in his life, huh? Guess you were wrong on that score," the kid said.

"Okay, okay, let's concentrate on what we're doing. Never mind about the horses." He could scarcely believe that maybe the cowboy was for real.

They found some loose boards at the rear and were able to squeeze inside. Ross shone his light around the almost empty shed until it came to rest on the canoe.

"Well, what do you know? My old friend, the canoe. We've been on many a scenic adventure together has this canoe and me."

"Never mind that, how are we going to get it out of here?" the kid asked.

Ross looked around. Except for the door, there was no other way out large enough to free the canoe.

"We're just going to have to take that door off its hinges," he said. "We might need a nail or a spike. Have a look around and see if we can find something to bang out the pins."

After a short search, Ross came up with a nail. "We should be able to knock out the pins with this."

After coming up with a rock, Ross approached the door and attempted to knock out the pins to free the door. After several attempts, the door fell inward and Ross smiled to himself. That cowboy wasn't so smart after all, he thought, as he moved toward the canoe.

"Let's get this thing loaded and get out of here," he said to the kid. "You take the front and I'll take the rear."

After some maneuvering, they managed to get through the door and were headed for the truck when the yard lights came on and someone yelled, "What's going on out there?"

"Oh no," Ross said. "Keep going and don't stop whatever you do," he told the kid.

"I didn't get paid for this," the kid said.

'You won't get paid at all unless we get this thing loaded and out of here."

"Where do you figure on going with that?" the cowboy yelled at them from his porch.

But Ross refused to stop. He was so close to getting his canoe back, after all he had gone through, that stopping was out of the question.

When he was within fifty feet of his truck, the cowboy was suddenly right beside him. How had he got there so quick? Was he an Olympic runner or something?

The cowboy stuck out his foot and Ross lost his balance and down he went, banging his head on the rear of the canoe and bouncing off before landing on his back. He lay there stunned for several seconds. The kid dropped his end of the canoe and disappeared down the road, running for all he was worth.

Ross attempted to stand up, but before he could regain his feet, he was immediately knocked down again. Blood rained down from his mouth where his face had hit the canoe and Ross knew that he had lost not only his chance to regain his canoe but also another tooth.

When he sat up, he could see the cowboy staring down at him, hands on hips and shaking his head. "Some thief you turned out to be," he said. "Now I suggest you get yourself out of here as fast as you can and don't come back. Next time you might not be able to walk away under your own steam."

As he limped toward his truck, Ross turned and looked back at the cowboy. He had won this round, he thought to himself, but he wasn't about to throw in the towel. That canoe belonged to him and he was determined to get it back no matter what the consequences.

Down the road a half a mile, he ran across the kid walking along, his head down, the picture of defeat. He was probably mourning the fact that he wasn't going to get the rest of the fifty dollars he was promised. Well, that was just too bad. If he had held up his end of the bargain, Ross *might* have stopped to pick him up and given him the additional twenty-five dollars, but there was no way he was going to do that now.

He heard the kid yell when he recognized the truck. But Ross just smiled and kept right on driving.

CHAPTER FOURTEEN

THE NEXT AFTERNOON JUST BEFORE THREE O'CLOCK AND after one of the most uncomfortable nights he had ever spent sleeping in his truck and enduring the pain from his mouth, Ross parked his truck outside the school and waited for Andy and his friend to emerge. He had spent most of the morning trying to recover from his spill after the cowboy had tripped him. He was sure he had a concussion never mind the loss of another tooth. He could scarcely move and when some kids looked into his truck and laughed when they saw him, he finally decided that maybe it was time to rouse himself and get his day started.

He was starving after not having eaten anything since the previous morning, but he wasn't sure he could chew anything considering the state of his mouth. About all he could eat was some porridge and maybe yogurt, although he had always hated yogurt with a passion.

He took out his wallet and checked his finances. He only had twenty-five dollars left. It was a good thing he didn't pay that kid the extra money or else he wouldn't even have enough to buy a sandwich.

He heard the three o'clock bell ring and slumped down in his seat so that when the boys came out, they wouldn't be able to see him. It was going to be relatively easy to follow them while they led him right to Janet. He couldn't wait to get his hands on her. And maybe he could get some cash out of her purse once he had finished with her. Not being able to get his hands on the canoe, he had to come up with another means of getting some cash and why shouldn't Janet be the one to give him that opportunity?

At exactly 3:05, the two boys came running down the stairs of the school and began walking along the sidewalk toward home.

"So, what did you learn today?" Wayne asked Andy as they walked along.

Andy laughed and gave him a push. "You sound just like my mom." he said. "As if we are empty vessels just waiting to be filled up with knowledge."

"Well, isn't that what we are?" Wayne laughed. "One of these days I'm going to copy down a list of everything I learnt and when Mom asks me that questions, I'm going to rattle off every little thing that we did that day including going to the washroom and wiping my bum. Wouldn't she be surprised?"

"I'm sure she would, especially going to the washroom. I'm never quite sure what parents expect us to say when they ask that? I guess they're just making conversation, huh, showing interest in their amazing offspring."

As they crossed the street, Andy looked back and then turned to Wayne. "See that beat up old truck creeping along behind us? I'll bet whoever's driving it, is following us. I noticed it because it started moving slowly as soon as we came out of the school. Looks a little suspicious to me."

"You don't suppose it's old Ross, do you, hoping to follow us and find out where my mom is?"

"I wouldn't put it past him," Wayne said. "But how would he know where to find us?"

Wayne stopped and seemed to be considering Andy's question. He noticed that the beat-up old truck had stopped too. "I'll bet he followed Mom and Dad home last night. They might have tipped him off about who they were."

"So, what are we going to do? We sure don't want to show him where Mom is working. Maybe we should cut across the park and try to lose him."

"I've got a better idea," Wayne said. "Let's go right over and talk to him. That ought to shake him up a bit. Let him know we're on to him. What do you think?"

"I think that's exactly what we should do. Let's go."

Before Ross had a chance to drive away, the two boys ran up to his truck. "Hey Ross," Andy said through the open driver's side window. "Fancy seeing you here? What's up?"

Ross gave him a sickly smile. "Nothing much. Just waiting for somebody. How are you doing anyway, Andrew? You going to that school back there?"

"Sure am. If you're looking for my mom, you're out of luck. She's working downtown in one of those fancy hotels and making pretty good bread. But if I were you, I'd steer clear of her. She's pretty mad at you."

"Mad at me? I should be the one..." He stopped himself and looked around. "I'm not looking for her. She and I are kaput. I'm finished with her. Sorry about that kid."

"What happened to your mouth, Ross? You look like you've been through a meat grinder."

"Just a little accident," he said. "Nothing serious."

"I'd say you're going to need some pretty serious dental work there. That could cost you a pretty penny."

"Say, I've got to be somewhere in a few minutes," Ross said, looking at his watch. "Nice running into you guys. Hope you're doing all right, Andrew. See you later." He peeled away, his tires screeching as he roared down the street barely missing some students walking at the side of the road.

"Now, don't you think he seemed a little anxious to get out of here?" Wayne said. "If that isn't a man with a lot on his mind, I'll be a monkey's uncle."

The two boys made their way to the Cozy Café with the help of the map Andrew had drawn. Andy was glad to see his mother, especially since she was now employed and doing work that she enjoyed.

'Hey Mom," he said to her after they had taken a seat in the restaurant and she came over to greet them. "Great to see you. How's the new job going?"

Janet sat down beside her son and gave him a hug. "It's going just fine. But how are you two guys doing?"

"We just had a…meeting with Ross in front of the school," Andy said. "I don't think he was happy to see us."

"You met him?" Janet said. "What was he doing at the school?"

"Hoping to follow us so he could track you down. But we sent him off on a wild goose chase. Hopefully, by now, he's downtown trying to locate you amongst some of the hotels there. That should keep him busy for a while. He sure looks rough though. That rock you dropped on his head did major damage to his mouth. His speech is a little mumbly these days and he's barely recognizable. He's definitely not the Ross of old."

Janet reached out and took Andy's hand. "You know, despite what he's done, I'm relieved I didn't kill him with that rock. I did a lot of soul searching over that. But maybe he'll get the message and leave us alone now."

"That's not likely to happen," Andy said. "Ross seems to have a one- track mind and that is to seek revenge at any price. You're going to have to be really alert, Mom. He's very dangerous."

Janet smiled. "Well, I'm not going to be entirely alone when it comes to Ross. I've got you guys looking out for me as well as my boss, Louis. He owns the restaurant and he's very protective. And he's not about to let anybody harass me, especially somebody like Ross."

While the two boys enjoyed some fries and a coke, Louis approached them, holding out his hand. "Hi guys, welcome to the Cozy Café. I'm Louis."

The boys looked at one another and then back at Louis. "Holy catfish," Wayne said, shaking hands with the owner. "Wait until old Ross gets a gander at you. He'll be so anxious to make his escape, he'll probably be tripping all over himself."

"We're counting on that," Louis said, chuckling. "But you never know about somebody like Ross. You might have to kill him before he gets the message."

The two boys laughed. "Now there's a solution I didn't think of," Andy said. "A little drastic maybe, but effective."

"Hopefully, we won't have to go to that length to discourage him," Louis said. "I really like your mom, Andy, and I would hate to lose her. She's very good at her job."

After Ross left the two boys, he drove downtown with the intention of doing a search of some of the hotels there in the hopes of finding Janet, but the more he thought about it, the more he was convinced that what the boys had told him was pure fabrication. For one thing, they were not walking toward home. It seemed more likely that they were heading toward a restaurant where Janet was working. In telling him about the hotels downtown, they were probably hoping to throw him off the scent and get him to waste his time looking without any hope of ever finding her there.

He pulled over and parked his truck and sat thinking about what his next move should be. He had to do something soon because his mouth was aching and he had to attend to that before it turned into something really serious. He knew that he should go to emergency and see a doctor, but right now there were more serious issues he had to attend to, specifically finding Janet and getting his canoe back.

The thought of that cowboy getting the best of him rankled him to no end. It wasn't just not being able to get the canoe back that bothered him, but the fact that the cowboy had bested him at every turn and seemed to enjoy seeing Ross make a fool of himself. Well, there was still one option open to him. He had previously been reluctant to make use of the option but there seemed no other way.

The law was on his side, he knew that. After all, the canoe belonged to him. He could identify it because he had carved his name on the underside of the bow. And not returning it to its rightful owner was theft, wasn't it? Ross knew he was right. He just didn't like the thought of involving the cops. The cops weren't his friends. But it was obvious that he had to report the theft to the cops and get them to confiscate it if he hoped to get his canoe back and be able to spit in the face of the cowboy. He chuckled to himself. How ironic was it, that here he was about to involve the cops when for most of his life, he had been trying his best to make himself scarce around them.

As for Janet, he was just going to have to continue visiting restaurants until he found her, and he would find her eventually. She couldn't dodge him forever.

An hour later, Ross found himself outside the Riverside Police Station after asking several people where the institution was. It struck him as amazing that several of the people he had asked, didn't have any idea where it was. He had bought a pair of horned-rimmed glasses in a dollar store and with his baseball cap pulled down over his eyes, he was certain that the cops wouldn't recognize him.

He entered, suddenly feeling as though he were about to give himself up for some imagined felony, but managed to shake it off and approach the man sitting at the desk.

"Yes sir, what can I do for you?" the pudgy cop at the desk asked him.

"I'd like to report a theft," Ross said.

"Your name?" the cop asked,

"Joseph Smith."

The man picked up a pen and began to write. "Article that was stolen?"

"A canoe, a very expensive canoe. Not one of those 400 dollar jobs from Walmart but a specialty. Cost me almost 25 hundred dollars."

"Color of the canoe?"

"Orange."

"Make?"

"Pelican."

"Place stolen from?"

"My place. Or at least where I used to live. I was forced to move but couldn't take my canoe. When I came back for it, the new renter wouldn't allow me to take it."

"What address are we looking at here?"

"400 Cedar Creek Road."

"Okay, I'll have a constable ride out there and see if we can't get your canoe back."

"Thank you, sir," Ross said, suddenly finding a new respect for the police. "When can I expect someone to go out there?"

"Hey Tom," the deskman said, "you got time to take a ride out to Cedar Creek Road to fetch a stolen canoe?"

Tom, a tall, middle-aged man with a grey moustache and a no-nonsense look about him, put on his cap and approached the bench. "Sure, what's the story?"

"Fellow here left his canoe at his old house and the new owner won't give it up. Maybe you could use your wonderful powers of persuasion to convince him to hand it over."

"No problem," the cop said.

"Can I ride out with you?" Ross asked him.

"Sure, why not?" He glanced at his watch. "Shouldn't take long and with my powers of persuasion," he winked at the deskman, "we should be back here in no time. What do you think, Harry?"

"You got my vote," Harry said.

"You got a truck?" Officer Tom asked. "You'll probably need it if your friend decides to hand over the canoe."

'Yeah. I'll follow you out," Ross said.

Fifteen minutes later, they parked outside Ross's former house. There was no sign of the canoe as the two men got out of their vehicles.

"Do you know this guy's name?" Officer Tom asked.

"Haven't a clue. All I know is that he's a cowboy with a real mean streak running right down the middle of his back."

"Well, let's see what he's got to say about it," Officer Tom said, leading the way up the path toward the front door of the house. "I'm pretty good at dealing with mean cowboys."

Before they got there, the cowboy appeared on the stoop shaking his head and looking as though he couldn't quite believe what he was seeing.

"You again? Man, you are persistent."

"This man claims you've got his canoe. Now it would be real nice if we can negotiate a settlement here and get this man's canoe back so that we can get out of your hair and get back to doing what we were busy with before all this happened. What do you think?" queried officer Tom.

"I already told him I don't have his canoe. Never saw it, don't have a clue where it is, and if I did, I would give it back to him. What do I want with a canoe?"

"Oh, come on," Ross said. "It was leaning right there against the house and it's got my name carved in it. Who do you think you're kidding?" He wasn't about to tell officer Tom about his attempt to steal it back. That little gesture might end up getting him into more trouble than he had bargained for.

"No idea what you're talking about," the cowboy said. "You must be having hallucinations if you think there's a canoe around here."

"It's probably in the shed back there," Ross said.

"Mind if we have a peek?" Officer Tom asked.

"Help yourself," the cowboy said.

Ross could see that the door had been put back on its hinges as they approached the shed. Once inside, it was obvious that there was no canoe in sight nor any sign that one had been there.

"I don't believe this. My canoe has got to be here someplace unless he took it off his property and has it stored somewhere else."

"I told you I don't have it," the cowboy said as he came up behind them. "Never had it, never laid eyes on it. I still think you're having hallucinations fella."

Officer Tom looked at Ross and shrugged his shoulders. "Not much I can do if there's no canoe here. Are you sure you got the right place?"

"I lived here for two years. I ought to know my own house. And I can tell you without a scintilla of a doubt that that canoe was here last night. This guy is pulling the wool over our eyes. He's a con man."

"Hey, watch who you're calling names," the cowboy said, putting his hands on his hips and glaring at Ross. "Else I'll have you up for slander."

"Whoa there you two, let's not let things get out of hand," Officer Tom said.

"I can't believe this guy. He steals my canoe and now he going to sue ME for slander. What a joke."

"Look," Officer Tom said, trying his best to be diplomatic, "if you've got his canoe you best fess up and turn it over. It's the honorable thing to do."

The cowboy laughed. "Like I already said, I never saw a canoe. This man is suffering from some kind of obsessive compulsive behavior. You can't believe a word he says."

"I'm sorry, Joseph, but there's not much I can do without the canoe in question being in evidence. You're just going to have to swallow this one I think."

"That canoe is around here somewhere," Ross said. The thought that he wasn't about to get it back was slowly beginning to dawn on him.

"Unless it's in my house or on my roof, or my horses are drinking out of it, it's pretty plain it's not here and never has been."

As Officer Tom turned and began making his way back to his patrol car, the cowboy smiled at Ross and winked. "Nice try, loser."

"Sorry I couldn't help you, Joseph," Officer Tom said, as they walked toward their vehicles. "I suspect your canoe is long gone, but I can't do much for you, my hands are tied, without seeing the canoe. You can still fill out a complaint at the office, but I don't think it'll do much good."

"I'd just like to get my hands around that guy's throat long enough to choke the truth out of him," Ross said.

"I don't think I would advise that," Officer Tom said. "I mean, we're only talking about a canoe here, right? Let's keep things in proportion. Besides, he looks awfully tough to me."

"I paid over two thousand dollars for that canoe."

Officer Tom shook his head. "My advice is just let it go. Sometimes we have to swallow our pride and admit defeat. It looks to me like this is one of those times."

CHAPTER FIFTEEN

When the two boys arrived back at Wayne's house, they found Mrs. Allison in the kitchen getting ready to prepare supper.

"My mom found a really good job as a waitress," Andy told her. "She likes her boss but I think she's still worried about Ross."

"That's good news about the job," Mrs. Allison said. "But let's hope Ross fades away somewhere and your mom can get on with her life."

"Yeah, it would be great if she can find an apartment. Then I could join her and get out of your hair."

"We love having you here, Andy. You're welcome to stay as long as you want. I just wish this thing with Ross would resolve itself somehow. It worries me with a man like that prowling around."

"He was waiting for us at the school hoping to follow us and find out where Andy's mom is," Wayne said. "But we sent him on a wild goose chase. Maybe we won't have to worry about him for a while."

"That man sounds positively crazy," Mrs. Allison said. "You would think the police could do something about him, wouldn't you?"

"I guess until he does something that's criminal, they wouldn't do anything," Andy said.

Later, when the two boys were in Wayne's bedroom, Andy turned to his friend. "You know, it would be really something if we could turn the tables on old Ross somehow. If he's going to be stalking my mom and making her life miserable, maybe we can stalk him, start doing a little damage, slow him down a bit. What do you think?"

Wayne laughed. "Now that sounds like something I would enjoy doing. But first we have to be able to find him. How are we going to do that?"

The two boys sat thinking.

"We could put something on Facebook," Wayne suggested. "Send him a little provocative message of some kind."

Andy shook his head. "Ross doesn't know a computer from a bar of soap. The only thing he's good at is watching TV."

"I wonder where he's staying?" Andy said. "I don't think he's got much money. He was always borrowing from my mom." He snapped his fingers. "I'll bet he's sleeping in that truck of his."

"Yeah, and that old truck of his sticks out like a neon sign."

"Maybe if we got on the bikes and rode around, we could find it. It might take a while, but I think it might be worth a shot."

The two boys did a high five.

"Let's get the bikes out and do a little reconnaissance," Wayne said. "You can ride my dad's bike. You never know what'll turn up."

"Supper is in about an hour, boys," Wayne's mom said.

Ross sat in his truck, his newly acquired binoculars stuck to his face. He had spent his last few dollars on them at a second-hand dealer. He had intended to steal them, but the proprietor had kept such a close eye on him that the opportunity hadn't presented itself.

His attention was trained on the waitresses inside the Cozy Café. He had decided that surveying the restaurant from a distance would probably be more productive. If he showed up at the door, Janet, if she was in there, would have an opportunity to see him first and disappear in the back until he left before resuming service to her customers.

He almost shouted for joy when he saw her. After all the cafes, diners, eateries, holes in the wall and restaurants he had visited and enduring the frustration of not being able to find her, he was finally rewarded for his patience.

There she was, the picture of efficiency, serving customers, smiling, talking and laughing, seeming to be enjoying herself just as though she had never tried to kill him by dropping a rock on his head. Obviously, she didn't have much on her conscience. Well, he would soon rectify that. The thought of confronting her, seeing the fear in her pert little face, gave him enormous satisfaction.

He watched her for several minutes, chuckling to himself, mentally patting himself on the back for his persistence in finding her. She might think she was clever in being able to evade him for several days, but he had caught up to her and she was going to pay big time for what she had done to him.

As Louis sat in his office looking out the window and feeling a sense of well-being, he heaved a sigh of satisfaction. He couldn't help smiling to himself. The restaurant was busy, he had an army of friends and he was getting married in just over a month to the girl of his dreams. What had he done to deserve such a good life?

There was a knock on his door and Andre, his chef and all around handy man entered. "Hey boss, thought I better give you a head's up. I was taking out the garbage and what do I see but some guy in an old beat-up truck out there with a pair of binoculars stuck to his face. He was so busy looking that he didn't even notice me. He seemed very interested in what was going on inside the restaurant though. Think he's up to no good?"

Louis stood up, put on his jacket and smiled at Andre. "Thanks for keeping an eye out. I know exactly who that is and he is definitely up to no good. Guess I'm just going to have to go out there and put the guy straight. What do you think?"

"Sounds like a good idea to me," Andre said. "Need any help?"

Louis shook his head. "This is a job I want to do on my own. I've been expecting this guy to show up sometime and what do you know, here he is." He chuckled. "I think I'm going to enjoy making his acquaintance."

Louis went out the back door and circled around behind Ross's truck. Sure enough, Ross was so busy looking through his binoculars that he didn't notice Louis approaching him.

Without hesitation, Louis yanked on the driver's side handle, pulled open the door and grabbed Ross by the lapels of his jacket. Effortlessly, he pulled Ross out of his truck and held him up in the air.

"Say, are you Ross McDonald?"

"Yeah, who wants to know? Let me go or I'll call a cop."

"Now that wouldn't be a nice thing to do when we're just getting acquainted. I'm Louis Leblanc. I own this restaurant that you are so interested in. We specialize in French cuisine, but I don't suppose you've got an appetite for that just now. And do you know what, I just hired a really nice waitress the other day by the name of Janet. You wouldn't happen to know her, would you?"

"Yeah, she's my common-law wife and she tried to kill me and she stole my car. I don't think you want somebody like that working for you, do you?"

Ross struggled to free himself from Louis's grip but he wasn't having much success. The guy was gigantic. What was he, a professional wrestler?

"That can't be the girl I hired. Why, she wouldn't hurt a fly and everybody likes her. In fact, she told me all about you, Roscoe, and what a nasty piece of work you are. Are you stalking her?"

"What? No. I'm just trying to...would you let me down. I can't explain myself while you're holding me up like this."

Louis lowered Ross to the ground, but kept a tight grip on him.

"I'm not stalking her. I'm just trying to..."

"You're stalking her," Louis said. "And stalking is against the law. Did you know that? I particularly hate stalkers, especially when they're stalking one of my best waitresses."

"I told you, I'm not stalking her, she –"

"Let me give you some good advice, Roscoe." Louis said, putting his face so close to Ross, he could smell Ross's breath. "If I hear about you even going near my waitress, do you know what I'm going to do?"

Ross looked up at the six foot eight, three hundred pound giant who had an unshakeable grip on him and shook his head.

"I'm going to break all your fingers, one at a time. Once that's done, you might find it difficult to get rough with Janet. In fact, you might find it difficult to drive this truck of yours, or go to the bathroom, or even shake somebody's hand without it hurting. Not a nice position to be in, Roscoe. Know what I mean?"

When Ross didn't say anything, just stared up at Louis, Louis smiled. "You don't look so good, Roscoe. I'd say that mouth of yours needs looking at real soon. What happened anyway? You run into a pile driver?"

"I told you, she tried to kill me. She…"

"Now you best not go around saying stuff like that, Roscoe. I've known Janet for several days now and she's just about the sweetest lady I've ever met. So, if I were you, I wouldn't be saying things about her that aren't true. Because if what you say should get back to me, I just might lose my temper and…well, you get the picture. Now, I suggest you get back into that truck of yours and drive away from here never to return. Got it?"

When he released Ross, Ross jumped into his truck and locked the door. He was breathing heavily from his exertion but refused to look back at Louis.

"Bye, bye, Roscoe," were the last words Ross heard as he peeled out of the parking lot of the restaurant. Two blocks away, he pulled over and sat looking out the windshield, his breath coming in spurts as he tried to relax. He could scarcely believe what had just occurred and swore to get revenge, both on Janet and that giant slob who owned the restaurant. If it was the last thing he would do on this earth, he would get even with both of them.

CHAPTER SIXTEEN

THE NEXT AFTERNOON WHEN WAYNE AND ANDY GOT home, they immediately got out the bikes and pedaled down the road looking for Ross's beat-up truck. Wayne had grabbed his pocket knife out of his drawer just in case he might need it. You never knew when you might need a weapon when you were up against somebody like Ross, he thought. He hoped, of course, that he wouldn't need it, that things wouldn't come down to that kind of violence. But you never knew.

Despite being on bikes, the two boys covered a big area, riding up and down tree lined streets, looking for the elusive truck. They hadn't discussed what they might do when they found it, but they were in agreement that taking things one at a time was about all they needed for now. Once they found the truck, then they could decide just what they would do.

"I sure hope he doesn't find out where my mom is working," Andy said as they rode along. "She's already nervous about the guy, but if he suddenly showed up at her restaurant, she would go ballistic."

"I think that boss of hers will put the run on Ross," Wayne said. "I don't think I would want somebody as big as he is chasing after me. He seemed pretty protective of his waitresses."

"Ross can be a very slippery character," Andy said. "Smarmy is a good word for him. He's always been able to talk himself out of trouble one way or another. But I think Louis has a pretty good grip on what's been going on. I don't think he'll be fooled by Ross one bit."

After an hour of pedaling up and down hills, the two boys stopped at a park, got off their bikes and went over to a fountain for a drink. Riding a bike was hard work and they had worked up a thirst.

As they sat on a bench, looking out over the lake, getting their second wind, Ross's truck drove by.

"There he goes," Wayne yelled and the two boys ran for their bikes. Keeping him in sight was difficult, but since he had to stop for traffic lights, the boys managed to spot him several minutes after first seeing him by the park.

"We're never going to be able to keep up with him," Andy gasped, "if he doesn't park that crate he's driving pretty quick. I've just about had it."

As Ross pulled well ahead of them and turned a corner, the two boys stopped, breathing heavily and knowing they were never going to catch up to him.

"Now what do we do?" Andy said. "We're no match for a truck. We're just going to have to find him parked somewhere I guess."

After catching their breath, they proceeded along the road and turned the corner, hoping they might catch sight of Ross's truck, but to no avail.

"Well, at least we know he's in the vicinity and hasn't left town," Wayne said. "I guess he didn't fall for our story about your mom working downtown."

"I wonder where he was going so fast?" Andy said. "He looked like he was in a hurry. Maybe we'll get lucky and that wreck of a truck will break down on him. By the look of it, I'd be amazed if it doesn't pack up in short order."

Several blocks later, they sighted the truck again. It was parked in someone's driveway and it soon became obvious why Ross had parked there. The house looked deserted. The lawn hadn't been cut for weeks and weeds were growing everywhere. Newspapers had piled up on the front step. The owners had obviously left in a hurry without worrying whether their property was looked after or not. It was the ideal setup for Ross, who had probably broken into the abandoned house and was sleeping there.

The boys grinned across at one another.

"Well, what do you know. Ross has found himself a home. Now isn't that just dandy," Wayne said. "That house is a perfect match for his truck."

Andy laughed. "Now all we have to do is figure out what to do next. We're going to have to be careful he doesn't see us. Maybe we should wait until it gets dark."

"Good idea. It should be dark in an hour or so." He took out his pocket knife and opened the blade. "Maybe we should make sure that he can't go anywhere in that truck of his. What do you think about four flat tires? That might slow him down a bit."

They pushed their bikes down the street laughing the whole way. Finding Ross so quickly after he had left them in his dust, gave them added incentive to finish what they had intended to do.

They dropped their bikes a block away and lay down on the grass waiting for darkness. Ross, they decided, was probably passed out inside the house, exhausted from trying to sleep in his truck. But they weren't going to take any chances of being seen and ending up in a confrontation with him. Although he was in rough shape, they were still no match for him.

When it was sufficiently dark, the two boys jumped on their bikes and rode toward Ross's truck parked in the driveway. Since no one lived in the house, there was no light around it, which made it almost impossible for Ross to see what they were doing, even if he happened to be looking out the window.

Wayne took out the pocket knife and systematically jabbed the blade into each of the four tires. Within minutes, the truck was a sad looking sight. It was now half a foot shorter and completely out of commission.

The two boys stood admiring their handiwork.

"I don't think Ross is going to be travelling very far in the next little while," Andy said.

As they ran toward their bikes, they did a high-five, shaking their heads and wondering how long it was going to take Ross to get back on the road.

"Since he's probably broke," Andy said. "He might just have to leave his truck and do some walking. And if I know Ross, he won't be walking very far. He never was much for that kind of exercise. Lifting weights was more his style."

The next morning when Ross came out of the deserted house and saw his truck, he could scarcely believe his eyes. He let out a scream that was loud enough to wake anybody in the vicinity out of a deep sleep.

"It's those kids. I'm going to hang them by their toes when I catch them. What a couple of little delinquents."

As he stood surveying the damage to his tires, he couldn't help wondering how they knew where he was. "Sneaky little beggars," he said to himself. Now what was he supposed to do? There wasn't even a spare in the truck, let alone four tires. It would cost him a pretty penny to call a tow truck let alone have the tires repaired, a pretty penny that he didn't have.

He sat down on the bumper of his truck and took out a cigarette. Just as he lit up, he saw an old man walking toward him from the house across the street.

"Howdy," the old man said. "You looking to buy this place? Or maybe doing some renovations? If you are, you got yourself a real project here. Place should be bulldozed."

Ross took a deep breath. This was all he needed right now. Some old codger wearing overalls and sporting a white beard that practically reached the ground sticking his nose in where it didn't belong. Ross was definitely not in the mood for company.

"Just doing some scouting around for a friend of mine," Ross said, wishing the old guy would turn around and go back where he belonged. He didn't want to have to explain anything to the old codger. "He's looking for a property he can improve. He likes buying up places like this and turning them into something special."

"Well, I wish him a lot of luck. Most folks around here would sure appreciate it if something was done to this place. It's a real blot on the neighborhood. Depreciates our homes and attracts a lot of riffraff. Don't know why city hall hasn't done something about it."

The old guy pointed at Ross's four flat tires. "It looks to me like somebody doesn't like you."

"You don't say," Ross said, taking a drag on his cigarette and then flicking it away. "Whatever would make you say that?" Maybe, he thought, if he was sarcastic, the old guy would go back to where he belonged.

"Saw the whole thing from my living room last night," he said. "Couple of teen-agers. Don't know what the next generation is coming to," he added. "Nothing but troublemakers if you ask me. Course I couldn't identify them if they were put in a lineup. It was pretty dark."

"I already know who's responsible," Ross said.

"Is that a fact?"

"And when I catch them, they're going to be very, very sorry."

The old man laughed. "They just get a slap on the wrist from the law," he said. "Sometimes taking the law into our own hands is the only way to get any justice."

"Don't know what I'm going to do now without my truck," Ross said out loud, talking to himself more than to his ancient visitor. He took out another cigarette wishing the old man would disappear. He didn't need company right now, he needed his truck with four good tires.

"I can help you with those tires," he said.

"Say what?" Ross said, suddenly seeing the old man in a different light. "How so?"

"Got a workshop in my basement. Give me a couple of hours and I'll have you back on the road again." He grinned at Ross and nodded his head. "I might be old, but I can still make myself useful. Worked for the railroad all my life until they finally let me go on my seventy-fifth birthday. I sure wasn't ready to retire. In fact, I was better at my job then than I was when I was younger. I needed that job, but they told me I was too old. Nice birthday present, huh? Now I just do odd jobs here and there to keep myself busy. I enjoy that."

"Say, that's real nice of you to offer to fix my flats," Ross said, suddenly changing his attitude and seeing the old man as being useful rather than a boring distraction. "But I'm afraid I can't pay you. I'm flat broke."

The old man waved his arms. "Don't need to be paid. Glad to do it for nothing. Helps fill in my day."

Ross could hardly believe his luck as he watched the old man cross the street to his garage. The old guy looked like he belonged in an institution for the aged. Was he really up to repairing four tires?

Ross watched as the old guy brought over all the equipment and went to work. He could hardly believe his eyes. He had never seen anybody, let alone a guy who looked just short of a hundred years old, do a job like he did. He was a marvel to watch. And he didn't want any help, he said. He had always worked on his own and found it more efficient that way.

A couple of hours later, Ross had four inflated tires on his truck and was back in business. The old guy took a little longer than he said, but Ross wasn't about to quibble about that. He still couldn't get over how efficiently the man went about his job.

"There you go young fella," he said when he was finished. "That ought to keep you on the road for a while." He chuckled and held out his hand. "Enjoyed meeting you. Hope you find those young rascals that did this to you."

Ross helped him carry his equipment back to his garage, shook his hand a second time and walked back to his truck.

It was time to get serious, he decided.

CHAPTER SEVENTEEN

AFTER LOUIS DEALT WITH ROSS AND WATCHED HIM AS he pealed out of the restaurant parking lot, he laughed to himself. What a dirt bag, he thought. And to think that Janet had actually lived two years with this guy. It was more than he could comprehend. Well, he hoped that he had scared him sufficiently to prevent him from bothering Janet. He hated guys that took advantage of women and saw them as weak little cowards who could never stand up to anybody their own size. But he had a sneaking suspicion that he hadn't seen the last of Ross. He knew the type. You practically had to bury them before they got the message.

When Louis returned to the restaurant, he signaled to Janet to follow him into his office.

"I just had a little run-in with your ex," he told her once they were seated across from one another. "He was watching you through a pair of binoculars."

"Oh no," Janet said. "I can't believe he's found me already. Now what am I going to do?"

"I put the run on him and gave him some quite unpleasant options if he continued to bother you, but he strikes me as being a hard man to scare off."

"You're so right. Once he sets his mind to something, nothing seems to deter him. I wonder how he found out where I'm working."

Louis leaned back and regarded Janet, thinking that maybe he should have broken one of Ross's fingers to convince him that he was serious.

"It was just a matter of time I think. There's not so many restaurants in this town that he wouldn't eventually find the right one." Louis sighed. "Well, it's up to you if you would like to continue working here knowing he knows where you are. I'll do whatever I can to persuade him to leave you alone."

Janet sighed deeply and looked out the window. "I want to keep this job. I'm really enjoying it and if I leave, he'll just find me again."

"Have you given any thought to where you might want to live? You must be tired of staying in that motel."

"I haven't. I've been so comfortable there with nobody bothering me and being able to walk to work. But I know, I have to find an apartment so Andrew, my son, can join me."

"I know a lady who owns an apartment block. She usually has one or two places for rent. Why don't I give her a call and see what she's got? Her apartments aren't that far away so you could still walk to work."

Janet shook her head. "You have been so kind to me, Louis. I do appreciate everything you've done for me. Yes, I would like to look at one of your friend's apartments. That would be great." She looked at her watch. "I would like to take Andrew with me when I look at it. It's important that he likes the apartment too. He said he was going to drop in after school with Wayne."

"OK, you go back to work and I'll call my friend. I guess you would be looking for a two bedroom. Right?"

"Right. And thank you so much, Louis." When he stood up, she went over to him and gave him a hug. "You're something else. I feel so fortunate to have met you."

"Hey, I feel privileged to have you working for me so it works both ways," Louis said. "And I don't want you harassed by the likes of Ross McDonald. Nobody deserves that kind of treatment. So, I'm just doing what comes naturally to me." He chuckled. "Sounds like the title of a song, doesn't it?"

As Janet resumed her duties in the restaurant, she couldn't help looking out the windows, fearing that Ross might well be out there this very minute watching her through his binoculars. She wondered whether she was ever going to be rid of the man. He had been making her life so miserable for so long, that perhaps she was doomed forever to having to constantly look over her shoulder. She wondered what Louis had said to him. She would love to have been a fly on the inside of Ross's car to hear what Louis had said. Whatever it was, it was probably not enough to discourage Ross, Ross being what he was and not easily frightened.

When Andy and Wayne appeared just before Janet's shift ended, Louis came out of his office and approached them.

After greeting the boys, he turned to Janet. "I called my friend. Her name is Beatrice and she said she has a couple of apartments available and to send you right over." He handed her a piece of paper. "I've drawn a little map to show you just where the apartments are. They're called Lion's View Estates. I think you'll like them."

"What do you think, guys? Want to help me with a little house-hunting? I could sure do with a second opinion."

The two boys looked eager. "Wow, Mom, that would be great. You must be getting tired of living in a motel. And I consider myself a pretty good judge of properties." He laughed. "They've got to be a big improvement on the last place we lived in."

"We're sure going to miss you, Andy," Wayne said. "In a way, I hope you hate the apartments." He poked his friend and laughed. "Just kidding."

"The apartment block is only about a fifteen- minute walk from here," Louis said. "I'll see you in the morning, Janet," he added, before going back to his office.

Janet felt safe walking with the two boys as they made their way toward the apartment block. Surely Ross wouldn't try anything while the three of them were together, she thought, although nothing would surprise her when it came to her ex-boyfriend. He was just about the most unpredictable person she had ever known and the most obnoxious.

"I don't think we've got much to worry about concerning Ross," Andy said. "At least for the time being. We kind of put him out of commission last night. It might take him a day or two to figure out how to get himself on the road again."

Janet couldn't help smiling and looked over at the boys with a kind of wonder. "Just what have you two been up to?" she asked. "No good, I bet."

"This is one time when being up to no good is a really good thing," Wayne said. "What do you think, Andy?"

Andy nodded. "Anything we can do to knock Ross off his pedestal has got to be good. I feel like one of those guys in a western who has a free hand to do what he likes no matter whether it's against the law or not."

"You've turned into a real desperado," Wayne said, laughing. "But it's a lot more fun than being law-abiding, wouldn't you say? Somehow, I don't think there's going to be an APB out on us in the near future."

"Ross and the police are like a cat and a mouse. He's got a lot in his background that we don't know about and that he would just as soon not publicize. But it sure would be interesting to know what he's been up to in the last few years."

Following the map that Louis had given them, they soon approached the Lion's View Estates which had a lion on each side of the stairs that led to the apartments.

"Hey, these are cool," Andy said, reaching out and petting one of the lions as they ascended the stairs.

Beatrice turned out to be a tiny woman under five feet tall but with a smile that reached almost across her face. Her white hair and brown eyes sparkled when she appeared at her door.

"Well, well, well," she said. "You must be Janet. And these must be your boys."

"Just one of them," Janet said, putting her arms around Andy. "The other one is his partner in crime."

Beatrice laughed. "Well, I have two apartments available, but I think only one of them would be suitable, so

The Homeless Stalker

I'll show you that one first. It's on the second floor and has two bedrooms. The other one is on the first floor, but I always think, especially for women on their own, that it's more secure for you being up higher."

As they walked through the apartment inspecting each room and trying to envision themselves living there, Andy couldn't help feeling as though this was the kind of place he would enjoy living in. Having his own room was a big priority compared to having to sleep on the floor on a foam mattress. Also, the lack of privacy in his old house had always been a bone of contention.

"What do you think, Andrew?" Janet said when they had completed the inspection.

"I love it," he said. "It's just perfect." He turned to Beatrice. "We'll take it. When can we move in?"

"Hey, just one minute there, young man," his mother said. "Who's renting this apartment anyway?"

"Oh," Andy said. "I guess I just got a little carried away. Sorry about that."

His mother laughed. "Guess I can't blame you considering what you had to put up with in our other place." She smiled over at Beatrice. "Nothing like youthful enthusiasm, is there?"

"I had four brothers. I know all about it."

"It might be a good idea if you boys went outside while Beatrice and I talk things over. Okay?"

"Okay," Andy said as the two boys left, clumping down the stairs and sitting outside beside the lions.

"Nice place," Wayne said, looking around at the abundance of hedges and trees and flowers. "I hope she takes it."

'Let's hope Ross doesn't discover where we are – at least for a while. I'm tired of having to deal with him and I'm always worrying about Mom. There's no telling what old Ross will do if he catches her somewhere by herself."

Fifteen minutes later, Janet came out wearing a smile and looking as though she had just won the lottery.

"I took it," she said. "I'm not sure how I'm going to pay for it on my salary, but let's worry about that later."

"Great," Andy said. "Wow, I can hardly wait to move in."

Half a block away, Ross smiled to himself as he watched through binoculars his one-time family doing high fives on the steps of the Lion's View Estates. What a pretentious place she had chosen. Who did she think she was, the Queen of Sheba? Besides, how could she afford a place like this on a waitress's salary?

"Did she think I wouldn't find out where she lived?" he said to himself. "She must be living in a dream world." Well, now that he knew where she was going to be living, he could take his time and think about how he was going to deal with her when the opportunity arose. What did you do with somebody who dropped a rock on your face? What penalty short of death could make up for that he wondered? He preferred sending her into the next world, but the thought of being caught and sent to prison for the rest of his life, didn't appeal to him. He had already spent enough time in jail to last him for the rest of his life.

He chuckled to himself thinking of what he might do to her. He could cut all her hair off. Women valued their hair more than anything else in this world and Janet was particularly vain about her hair. She would hate that. And he could give her a couple of black eyes and a broken nose. That big oaf of a boss of hers might not be so keen to keep her if she showed up looking like a zombie.

He shook his head just thinking about Louis. What a great big ugly oaf he was, Ross thought, full of empty threats. If he ever did break even one of his fingers, Ross would sue him for everything he had. In fact, he might even end up owning that fancy little restaurant of his. Now wouldn't that be a nice piece of justice?

An hour later, Ross lay on the grass, his binoculars stuck to his face, staring in at his former residence. He was certain that his canoe was somewhere on the property and when the cowboy left in his fancy truck, Ross was going to have a look around. There were several acres where the cowboy could hide the canoe and Ross meant to find it one way or another.

After Ross had lain on the grass for half-an-hour, the cowboy came out of his house, got in his truck and drove away. Ross gave it a good five minutes before getting on his feet and walking toward the house. It didn't look as though he had locked the place up so it might be easy getting inside. He didn't think the canoe was in the house, but he meant to check it out just to make sure.

As he made his way up the steps and toward the front door, he turned and looked behind him, just in case the cowboy forgot something or was on a quick trip. Then he reached for the front door and pushed it open.

It was dark inside and stiflingly warm. Ross made his way across the room, wondering if there was anything of value he might be able to pick up while he was here. He didn't feel one ounce of guilt since the cowboy had stolen his canoe and owed him big time anyway.

"Who are you?" a voice suddenly broke the silence.

Ross almost jumped out of his skin. He turned toward the voice and could just see an elderly woman sitting in a rocking chair with a shawl over her.

"Cat got your tongue?" the woman said. "I asked you who you were."

"Ah...I'm a friend of your...son's," Ross stammered.

"He doesn't have any friends and he's not my son. He's my grandson. What, you think I had him when I was sixty-five years old? He's just a kid without a brain in his head. Anyway, what are you doing here? Do you make a habit of walking into people's houses without being invited?"

"Your grandson has my canoe. I was hoping to pick it up."

"Canoe? What canoe? There's no canoe around here. My grandson wouldn't know one end of a canoe from the other."

"I used to live here before you moved in. I left my canoe behind. I need to get it back."

"Let me give you some good advice, young man," the old lady said. "Myron is going to be back real soon. He went to the drug store to pick up a prescription for me. He's got a real temper and he's mean. If he catches you in here, I can't be responsible for what he'll do to you. He's tough. He might not be the brightest penny around, but I sure wouldn't want him mad at me."

Ross went to the window and looked out just in time to see Myron's truck pull into the driveway.

"I got to get out of here," he said, heading toward the back door. "Don't tell him I was here."

"We ain't exactly on speaking terms right now," the old lady said. "So, rack one up for you." She laughed as she watched Ross disappear out the rear door.

When Myron opened the front door, his grandmother screamed. "There was some guy here. He just walked right in uninvited. Scared the life out of me. Said you had his canoe."

"What? I can't believe it. Where is he?"

"He just ran out the back door this minute."

When Myron returned to the front door, he could see Ross running toward the road. "I'm going to teach that guy a lesson," he said, running down the steps and pursuing Ross.

Ross had a good hundred-yards lead on him, but his truck was at least a quarter mile down the road. He wasn't sure he could outrun Myron in his condition. He hadn't eaten much in the last few days and was so hungry that morning that he had driven into town and had finally, out of desperation, gotten something to eat at the Salvation Army soup kitchen.

When he looked over his shoulder, he could see Myron gaining on him. The kid was a lot younger than Ross, at least ten years, and looked to be in good shape. There was no way he wanted to get into a tussle with the guy. He was at least six inches taller than Ross and probably fifty pounds heavier.

He could see his truck up ahead, but Myron was right on his tail. Realizing that he wasn't going to make it to the safety of his truck, Ross stopped, breathing heavily and about ready to throw up. He turned to face Myron.

He put up his hands. "All right, all right. You win. I give up. You can keep the canoe. I don't want it any more. It isn't worth it."

"Never mind the canoe," Myron said, coming right up to Ross and pushing him hard. "You scared the daylights out of my gran."

"Sorry about that," Ross said. "I didn't mean to. I didn't even know she was there."

"And that's another thing," Myron said, shoving him again. "Entering our house without being invited. That's a felony. You could go to jail for that. It's called breaking and entering."

"I didn't break anything."

"Doesn't matter. You scared my gran. That's worse than breaking something."

He walked over to Ross's truck and kicked one headlight and then moved over to the other one and kicked it. "Where did you get this wreck anyway?" He laughed. "What a piece of junk. I think I improved it by kicking out its lights."

"How about we just call it even," Ross begged. "You get the canoe and I get out of here never to come back."

"I lent that canoe to a friend and he racked it up going down some rapids. It's probably in a million pieces by now, lying at the bottom of a river."

Ross shook his head, thinking of all the times he had come out here and now his beloved canoe no longer existed. What a waste of time and energy and a lot of frustration dealing with this cowboy. He would like nothing more than to knock the guy into next week but he knew that wasn't going to happen. He was too weak to beat up on anybody, least of all a tough, well-conditioned brute who was probably ten or fifteen years younger than him. There was a day when he might have been able to handle this guy but now wasn't that time.

Ross got into his truck and watched as the cowboy, his arms crossed and smiling as though he had just won first prize in an arm wrestling contest, stood in the middle of the road almost daring Ross to run over him. There was nothing Ross would enjoy doing more, but he was already in enough trouble with the law without adding to it.

He stuck his head out the side window and said, "Is your name really Myron?"

"Yeah, so what?" Myron snapped.

"God, I wouldn't give my dog a name like that," Ross said. When Myron started toward the truck, Ross put it in gear and pealed out of there before Myron could lay hands on him. It gave him a particular satisfaction to have the last word with this cowboy who had gotten the better of him so many times.

Ross drove back to the abandoned house where he had been sleeping for the last few nights and parked his truck in the driveway. When he got out, he could see his friendly neighbor leaving his verandah and coming over to talk to him. Although he appreciated the old guy for repairing his four tires, he wasn't in the mood for company of any kind. All he wanted to do was lay down somewhere and lick his wounds and have something to eat. Unfortunately, he had no food and he was out of money.

"What happened to your headlights?" the old man wanted to know.

Ross sighed. He didn't have the energy to even give the old man a reason. He just sat down on the steps of the abandoned house and hung his head. "You wouldn't happen to have a beer, would you?" he asked.

"A beer?" He looked back toward his house. "I might have one in my fridge. You thirsty?"

"I'm dying of thirst," Ross said.

"I'll see what I've got," he said. "I'm not much of a drinker myself, but my wife likes a beer now and again."

He returned to his house and reappeared several minutes later carrying a beer. "It might be a little flat," he said, handing it to Ross. "It's been sitting in the fridge for a while, but it's cold and wet."

Ross had never tasted anything so good in his whole life as he consumed the beer in one long draft. "Thanks," he said. "I appreciated that."

"You figuring on sleeping in this house tonight?" the old man asked. When Ross nodded, the old man shook his head. "Might not be a good idea. The cops were around today. The neighbors have been complaining about this place. Been a lot of shady-looking characters camping out in this place lately, probably selling drugs and doing god knows what else. They told me they would be back later on tonight."

"Oh no," Ross said, thinking that now he was going to have to spend another night sleeping in his truck somewhere. The thought did not please him.

"I'd offer you a bed in my basement, but the wife, she wouldn't be pleased. She's suspicious of everybody. Thinks anybody who would camp out in this old house is a crook ready to relieve us of everything we own. But I could see you were different owning a truck and all."

Ross had to chuckle to himself. If the old guy knew what Ross had been up to in the last few days, he might not be so trusting. He held out his hand. "Thanks for the beer old timer. Sure did appreciate it. And I think I might take your advice and beat it out of here. Don't fancy mixing it up with the cops."

"Don't blame you there," the old man said. "Nice meeting you. Don't take any wooden nickels."

CHAPTER EIGHTEEN

"We're sure going to miss you," Mrs. Allison said to Andy. "We've enjoyed having you here. You're just going to have to come over often and see us."

Andy looked over at his new-found friend, Wayne. "It's been great and if Mom didn't need me so badly, I would consider staying right here. But with Ross out there somewhere with murder in his heart, I feel scared to leave her on her own. It's been fun having a friend who is just like a brother."

"Yeah, we enjoyed giving old Ross four flat tires, didn't we?" Wayne said, taking out his jack knife and waving it at his mom. "We sure had him going for a while."

"Wayne, you didn't!" When Wayne laughed, and winked at Andy, his mother glared at him. "You have no idea what that man might do if he caught you. From what I saw of him, he's a very dangerous person."

"He's a very wounded person," Andy said. "From what I could see, he looks like he's on his last legs. He can hardly talk, his mouth is so mangled. You would think he would realize what a fool he's been and give it up before he collapses altogether."

"People like Ross never give up," Mrs. Allison said. "They're maniacs and have a one-track mind. That's one good reason why you shouldn't be fooling with him. He's likely to do anything to you."

"That's why I want to go and live with my mom. If I was there, at least we might have a fighting chance against him if he ever showed up at her apartment. Louis, her boss, has already threatened Ross if he goes near my mom, but in the meantime, Ross could do a lot of damage. I hope maybe I could help Mom. Between the two of us, we might be able to fight him off until Louis showed up."

Mrs. Allison left the couch and walked over to her son. She put her arms around his neck and forced him to look her in the eyes.

"Wayne, you must promise me that you aren't going to fool with that man. He's much bigger and stronger than you are and I don't want you hurt or maimed because you got in a tussle with a maniac. Do you understand?"

Wayne nodded reluctantly. The thought of helping his friend and getting the better of Ross appealed greatly to him, but his mother looked so serious that he knew he would have to heed what she said.

"What if he attacks us and we don't have a choice?" Wayne said. "What do we do then?"

"You run like hell," his mother said. "I'm pretty sure you can outrun him."

Ross was both hungry and thirsty. He had no money and his credit card had long since been maxed out. He longed for a hamburger and fries and a milkshake. His mouth watered when he thought about them. The thought of going back to the soup kitchen at the Salvation Army didn't appeal to him. He needed real food. Chewing it was going to be difficult, but it would be worth it.

He decided that the only way he was going to be able to get what he wanted was to order it and then walk out without paying. He had done it before tons of times. One more time wasn't going to be a big deal. And once he had settled up with that little tart of an ex-girlfriend of his who had tried to murder him, he would be long gone and be able to concentrate on getting a job and earning some money. He still chafed at the thought of not being able to get his canoe back. It was worth a lot of money and after selling it, he would have been in the pink, at least until he got a job.

It was going to be dark in an hour and he knew he couldn't be driving around without any headlights. That was sure to attract the cops and he didn't need them breathing down his neck.

He found a restaurant downtown, parked his truck near the entrance and entered. He sat at a table near the front door for a quick exit, ordered his hamburger and fries and luxuriated in their very smell when the waitress finally dropped them in front of him. God, he couldn't remember enjoying a meal like this in his whole life. It was like a banquet with all the trimmings. Better than Christmas, New Years and Thanksgiving all rolled into one, despite it hurting him when he chewed.

"Hey Ross, how are you? Haven't seen you around for a while."

Ross almost choked on his food. He hadn't expected to run into anybody he knew, but standing beside him was a guy he had worked with for several months, accompanied by a young woman.

Ross stood up, tried his best to smile and stuck out his hand. "Eddie. How are you? Fancy running into you."

Eddie was staring at him with a strange look on his face. "You get into a fight or something. Your mouth looks like somebody took a meat hook to it."

Ross laughed. "It's nothing, really. Just a little accident. It looks worse than it is."

"It looks pretty awful," Eddie said. "Shouldn't you have a doctor look at it?"

"My doctor's out of town. I'm waiting for him to return. Meanwhile, I'm just going to have to grin and bear it." He laughed, trying his best to appear nonchalant. "Pardon the pun."

"This is my fiancé, Sara. We're getting married next month."

Ross shook hands with the young lady, who was tall, blond and very pretty. She smiled at Ross. "Nice to meet you," she said. "I'm always interested in meeting Eddie's friends."

"Mind if we join you?" Eddie asked, pulling out a chair before Ross had a chance to reply. They both sat down and regarded him with interest.

Ross looked around, wondering how he was going to be able to get himself out of this predicament. It was beginning to get dark and he knew he would have to find somewhere to park for the night. Also, how was he going to walk out without paying with these two uninvited guests sitting beside him? He remembered Eddie was a real pain in the butt, always talking about how smart he was and how much money he was going to make. Ross didn't relish spending any more time with him or his girlfriend than he could help.

"So, what have you been doing with yourself since I last saw you?" Eddie asked, grinning at him as though he was his best friend when as far as Ross was concerned, he disliked the guy with the kind of intensity that one dislikes doing the laundry or taking out the garbage.

"Oh, this and that. I'm kind of between jobs right now."

"How's Janet doing? What a great girl. I used to envy you having such a sweet girlfriend, but now that I've met Sara, well, I'd say I'm pretty lucky too, don't you think?" He gave Sara the most nauseating smile Ross had ever witnessed.

Ross was desperate to finish his meal. It was getting cold and he was still starving. He looked down at his food and took a deep sigh.

"Look, I really have to go. It was great seeing you again. Congrats on your engagement and all that. Hope it all turns out well."

"But you're not finished your hamburger," Sara said. "We're not chasing you away, are we?"

"I'm not really that hungry," Ross said, looking down at his hamburger and cursing that he was about to leave most of it on his plate when he was so desperately hungry. Anyway, his mouth was so sore he wasn't even sure he could finish it.

He stood up, looking around, hoping the waitress wasn't going to show up with his check. It was getting darker by the minute as he looked out the window of the restaurant. He had to go and he had to go now.

"I'll give you our phone number," Eddie said, taking out a pen and writing a number on a napkin. He handed it to Ross. "Just give us a call when you can. We'd love to have you come to the wedding."

Ross was getting desperate. He headed for the door, giving them a wave.

"Aren't you going to pay for your meal?" Eddie yelled after him. Ross disappeared out the door and headed for his truck ignoring Eddie's attempt to get his attention. Once inside his truck, he turned the key but there was nothing but a click. He tried again with the same result.

Suddenly, Eddie was at his window. All the air went out of Ross's lungs as he rolled down his window.

"You didn't pay for your meal," Eddie said, looking distinctly less friendly than he had a few minutes earlier. "You didn't expect us to pay for it, did you?"

'No, no, of course not. I...I..."

"You weren't intentionally running out to avoid paying, were you?" Eddie asked. "I can't believe you would do that."

"Actually, I am a little short on cash," Ross said lamely. "If you could pay it, I would pay you later...when I come to your wedding."

"I think you'd better forget that, pal." He turned and went back into the restaurant. Ross tried starting the truck again, but all he could get was an annoying click.

"It must be the battery," he said to himself. "It's got to be the battery."

He got out and raised the hood. It was almost dark now and he had difficulty locating the battery in the dim light. When he finally did locate it, the posts were covered with corrosion.

"Sir, you didn't pay your bill," a female voice said and Ross took his head out from under the hood and looked at the woman standing before him. She didn't look pleased. "I'm the manager. I'm presuming that not paying your bill was an oversight."

"Yes, of course. And I'm terribly sorry," he said, giving her his patent smile. "Actually, I...I forgot my wallet. Can I come in tomorrow and pay it? There will be a nice tip for you."

"What's your name?" she asked.

"Ross McDonald. I'm good for it. You can trust me."

The waitress folded her arms. "Okay, Mr. McDonald. I'll expect to see you tomorrow without fail." She turned and re-entered the restaurant, looking back at him and shaking her head. He knew that she knew that she wasn't going to see him again any time soon.

Ross returned to his battery, twisted the cables around and cleaned the corrosion that had accumulated around the posts and then got back into his truck. He gave a little prayer as he turned the key and mercifully, the truck roared to life.

Ross took a deep breath and backed out. It was almost entirely dark now and he knew that he would have to find somewhere to park nearby if he was going to avoid running into the cops. God, what kind of luck was that running into old Eddie and his girlfriend? he thought as he roared out of the parking lot and headed down the street. Eddie was such a dork. What in the world could that blond have seen in him? He could tell her a thing or two about Eddie that might make her change her mind about marrying the guy.

He was still hungry having only eaten part of his meal. If he hadn't been in such a hurry to get out of there, he could have wrapped what was left in a napkin and brought it with him. But it was too late for that now. He was just going to have to wait until the morning and drive into town to the soup kitchen at the Salvation Army.

He received several honks from other cars as he drove along looking for an inconspicuous place to park where nobody would bother him. He found the ideal spot, pulled over and turned off his truck grateful that he hadn't run into the cops.

He was exhausted and didn't look forward to sleeping in his truck again. What had transpired over the last hour had left him strung out and he knew he wasn't going to be able to sleep a wink. He thought about Janet about to live in a nice apartment and here he was camped out in his car. How fair was that? As far as he was concerned, everything that had happened to him was her fault and he meant to even things up no matter what it took. He had spent two years with her and her rotten kid, doing his best to make a life for them, and this was the way she repaid him. Well, it was reckoning time and he could hardly wait. Seeing her happy at her work and earning wages while he roamed around the town like a lost puppy - that wasn't going to continue much longer. He deserved better. Hadn't he worked hard to try to make the bitch happy? And how was he repaid? She tried to kill him just as though he was a piece of garbage. He finally fell asleep from shear exhaustion and the comforting thought of finally getting his revenge.

CHAPTER NINETEEN

"Do you think your mom will be safe in her new apartment?" Wayne asked Andy as they prepared to go to bed. "Ross doesn't strike me as a guy who gives up easily."

"No I don't," Andy said. "And he's likely to do anything to her. I just hope I'll be there when he decides to make his move. I think between me and my mom, we should be able to prevent him from doing any damage."

"If you want, I'll stay over with you guys for a while. Three against one sounds like pretty good odds."

Andy laughed. "In his condition, I think I could handle him by myself. I'm surprised he can even walk let alone do any damage to anybody. He sure does look ugly, doesn't he? Enough to give a little kid nightmares." He sat considering Andy's proposal. "I don't want to take you away from your family, Wayne. Besides, Ross is probably going to be on the lookout and if he sees us going into my mom's apartment, he probably won't do anything anyway."

"He has to do something quickly I'd say," Wayne suggested. "You said he didn't have any money. How is he living being broke like that?"

"Old Ross is a pretty resourceful character so we shouldn't underestimate him. He can be quite charming and charismatic when he wants to be. Sometimes I think he could sell snow to the Eskimos."

"If he's so charming, how come he isn't rich?"

Andy laughed. "Because he's such a jerk. He's never held a job for more than a few months because he was always finding fault with whoever was giving him orders. My mom said he has a lot of difficulty with authority. I think he believes that he should be the king of the world."

"Your mom must have had it tough living with him," Wayne said.

"He would hardly let her out of his sight. A real control freak. I think he broke my mom's spirit. It was hard seeing what he was doing to her and not being able to help her."

The next day at work, Janet mentioned to Louis that she had taken one of the apartments that Vivian had shown her the previous day.

"It's an open plan and it will be wonderful having Andrew live with me again — especially without the interference of Ross to make our lives miserable."

"Don't forget, I'm available twenty-four-seven if that guy ever even comes close to you." He gave her a cell phone. "I don't use this any more so you can have it. Just give me a call. I'll fix him up real good. I'm not about to let anybody, let alone a bum like him mess with you. That guy should be in jail, not roaming around making a nuisance of himself.

"By the way," he added, "when are you going to be moving in?"

"Just as soon as I can," Janet said. "The sooner the better."

"I can round up a few guys to help you move. Just give me the word."

Janet laughed. "I haven't got any furniture so moving isn't going to be much of a problem. I guess we'll be sitting on the floor and eating off cardboard boxes for the first few days."

"I've got a garage full of old furniture, even a couple of beds. You can come over and pick out what you want. I've been meaning to donate it or have a yard sale, but have been putting it off. Most of it is still in pretty good condition. It ought to do until you can get around to buying some nice stuff."

"That would be wonderful," Janet said, shaking her head. "You know, I'm just never going to be able to repay you for all your kindness."

"Who needs repayment," Louis said. "Just having you here doing a great job is all the payment I need."

When Ross woke up the next morning and looked out his truck window, he felt a depression that seemed to engulf his whole body. He ached everywhere, especially his mouth, and he was hungrier than he had ever been in his life. When he switched on the ignition, he could see that the fuel needle was virtually on empty. He wasn't going to be able to get very far and would probably run out of gas before he could get downtown to the soup kitchen. And he still had to do something about those broken headlights which restricted his movements after dark.

Running out of that restaurant the night before had been a nightmare scenario, something he didn't want to repeat, but filling up his gas tank would be easy in comparison. It was just a matter of making his license plate obscure enough to be unreadable so that when he drove away without paying, the security cameras wouldn't be clear enough to read.

Well, he decided, this whole episode with Janet wasn't going to last forever. He would have to make his move in the next few days and then he would be gone, never to return. Losing his canoe still irked him, but he knew that he was going to have to write that one off. Dealing with that cowboy was one of the most dispiriting things he had ever experienced in his life. It wasn't often, he thought, that somebody, especially somebody that young, was able to get the better of him. He had always come out on top when dealing with the public. Most people were easily manipulated and naïve to the extreme which made dealing with them child's play. Unfortunately, that hadn't been the case with the cowboy.

He got behind the wheel of his truck and started it up, pulled out onto the road and drove away, keeping his eyes open for a service station where he could easily get free gas. He chuckled to himself. Sometimes life could be so simple.

That afternoon Andy and Wayne rode around on their bikes keeping an eye open for Ross's truck. If he was still determined to get revenge on his mom, Ross would have to be somewhere in the neighborhood of the apartments waiting to pounce. Once they spotted him, they could determine what action they wanted to take. Four flat tires had slowed him down. Maybe this time, they would have to do something more drastic.

"What do you think, Andy? Short of blowing up his truck, what do you think we can do?"

"Hmm. Well, let me see. Smash his windshield, put sugar in his gas tank, steal his rotor. Any of those appeal to you?"

"All three of them actually. But it might be hard to do any of them if he's in his truck. He's bound to be on the alert after getting his tires punctured. Hey, Andy, maybe we should get your mom a gun. It wouldn't have to be a real one with bullets. Just a toy maybe, that looks like a real gun."

"My mom doesn't like guns of any kind, toy or otherwise. I was thinking of something a little less lethal, like a baseball bat or a fireplace poker."

"Hey, we've got some dowelling in our garage. Dowels would make a nice light weapon. I think they're about an inch or two thick and about four feet long. You could do a lot of damage with one of those. And they're light enough so your mom could use one."

The two boys did a high-five, certain that they had found the perfect solution.

CHAPTER TWENTY

After Janet's shift at the restaurant, Mr. Allison and the two boys picked her up and they drove over to Louis's place to see if Janet could use any of the furniture stored in his garage.

"You're welcome to take anything you want," he said as they walked along the path at the rear of his house toward his garage. "It's all good stuff and I've been meaning to deal with it, but I just haven't got around to it."

Janet was hardly able to believe her eyes when she saw all the stuff Louis had just laying around. She was almost immediately able to find several items that she could make use of. There was a bed that had to be put together. She was pretty sure the boys could handle that without any trouble. Also, an old dresser that could easily be sanded and varnished and made to look like new. There were several book cases that would come in handy as well as several carpets. There were two tables and at least six chairs that matched one of the tables. She found an old couch and two matching chairs in a corner covered by some plywood and two by fours.

"Wow!" Janet said. "This is wonderful. "I'm not going to have to buy much at all – at least for a while."

Andy picked up a magazine rack. "Hey, I think you might be able to use this."

Janet laughed. "Well, I might have to wait awhile before I get any magazines, but I'm sure it'll come in handy later on."

Once Janet had everything picked out that she wanted, Mr. Allison brought his truck around to the back and they began loading the furniture.

"I don't know how to thank you, Louis. This is just wonderful." She laughed. "It seems I'm always thanking you for something. I just hope I'll be able to return the favor sometime."

"No need for that," Louis said. You just keep on being my best waitress and I'll be one happy boss. Besides, I much prefer giving this stuff to you. It's all still serviceable and needs a home."

Before they pulled away with the furniture, Louis's face suddenly took on a serious mold. "Say, that guy Ross – he hasn't shown his face around you lately, has he?"

Janet shook her head. "Nobody's seen him lately," she said. "We can always hope he's left town or given up on me but somehow I doubt that. Ross has got a one-track mind and he isn't easy to discourage."

"Well, don't forget. I'm on your side. If he shows up, let me know right away and I'll do my best to persuade him to leave you alone. I can only imagine what being stalked is like. Stalkers are crazy people that you can't reason with. They need to be stomped on. I'll keep an eye open myself. If he shows up around here, I just might have to point out the evil of his ways to him."

Ross found the perfect place to park his truck and still have an excellent view of the apartment complex where Janet now lived. He was able to drive his truck amongst a stand of trees and high grass so that it couldn't be readily seen from the road unless you were looking right at it. With his binoculars, he could quite safely observe Janet and her helpers as they moved her furniture into the apartment complex.

"What a fool," he said aloud. "Wasting her time moving all that stuff into an apartment when she's not going to be in any condition to make use of it once I get finished with her. More likely she'll either be in the hospital or up there shaking hands with Saint Peter."

Ross had developed a tic that bothered him almost as much as the festering around his mouth and teeth. His head ached and kept him from sleeping for more than a few minutes. He was relieved that at last he had arrived at the day of reckoning. Little did Janet know what awaited her. If she knew, she wouldn't be bothered carting all that old furniture into her apartment.

He sat smoking a cigarette, his one pleasure in life besides the thought of getting revenge on Janet. He was out of money but had managed to steal several packs of cigarettes at a corner store while the clerk was serving someone else. The cigarettes helped to quell his hunger. He would have done anything for a cold beer, but stealing a case of beer was a greater challenge than stealing cigarettes. Maybe he should have gone back to the old man's place. He was quite certain the old guy would have given him another beer.

Tomorrow at this time, he would be miles away from here. He wasn't sure where he was going, but wherever it was, it had to be a better place than where he was now. He had always been able to find a job no matter where he went being a jack of all trades kind of guy. It didn't matter to him what kind of work it was, as long as it paid well. He knew he was going to have to see a doc about his mouth and a dentist. How he was going to pay for that, he didn't know, but unless he had someone examine him, it was going to just get worse and he might end up in the hospital.

He got out of the truck and walked to the road to get a better look at the apartment complex through his binoculars. They were almost finished carrying in all the stuff. They were just like one big happy family. Now wasn't that just so sweet?

Ross returned to his truck and lay down across the front seat. He was exhausted and ached all over and was desperate for a good night's sleep. He closed his eyes, but sleep wouldn't come. It would be dark soon, he thought. Maybe then, he could get a few winks before setting out on a reconnaissance, looking to see where he could enter the building and discover which apartment Janet occupied. It was going to be so easy, like taking candy from a baby. It looked like he might have to deal with Andy first, but the kid was such a wimp, it was doubtful he would put up much of a fight.

CHAPTER TWENTY-ONE

When Janet arrived at work the next morning, she was met by Louis. He seemed particularly jolly as he led Janet into his office.

"So, how was your first night in your new apartment?"

"It was wonderful," Janet said. "The two boys stayed over and they were a great comfort. I think they were afraid to leave me alone with the thought of Ross being out there somewhere." She smiled with relief. "But there was no sign of him thank heavens."

Louis laughed. "Well, perhaps he's learnt his lesson. Some people take a while to figure it out. And some never figure it out at all. Let's hope Ross is amongst the former."

"It's so nice to have my own place at last and to see Andrew happy again and with a new friend. All the money in the world can't buy that kind of happiness."

"Well, I'm very pleased," Louis said. "And anything I can do to help, don't hesitate to ask. I'm always at your service."

Janet shook her head. "You are indeed my Guardian Angel," she said. "I don't know what I would have done without you."

"Haven't ever considered myself an angel," Louis said, smiling broadly, "but it's a nice thought."

After two weeks had passed and there was no sign of Ross, Janet began to breathe easier. Either Ross had left town permanently or had simply decided that the best thing to do was to let sleeping dogs lie, she didn't know, but she really didn't care. As long as he left her and Andrew alone, that was all she hoped for.

However, when she arrived at work one morning, Louis gave her a copy of the local paper, led her over to a booth and grinned down at her. "There's an article in there," he said, pointing to the paper, "that just might interest you."

Janet had no idea what Louis might be referring to as she glanced down at the newspaper. Louis pointed at an article at the bottom of the first page.

MAN FOUND IN HIS CAR AT THE BOTTOM OF A RAVINE

A man was found deceased in his truck at the bottom of Ashton Ravine by two boys who were playing in the area and made the discovery. It is thought that the truck had been there undiscovered for several weeks. Police have surmised that the decedent had parked his truck at the edge of the ravine amid a stand of trees with the intention of doing some reconnaissance of the area. They believe that the decedent was unaware of the ravine behind him and as his truck slid backward in the mud when he released the emergency brake, it plunged down the ravine where it remained undiscovered.

Police believe that there was no foul play involved but are puzzled by several circumstances. What was the decedent doing in that unusual and dangerous area? The fact that there was a pair of binoculars and a litter of cigarette butts in the cab of the truck indicated that the decedent was likely keeping a watch on the apartment complex directly below the hill. But for what purpose?

The decedent's emaciated body had undergone some quite severe injuries to his face and teeth, both of which would have needed immediate attention. The most unusual occurrence was *the fact that the decedent had several broken fingers on his right hand. Whether these injuries occurred when his truck went over the ravine is yet to be determined.*

Anyone who can cast any light on this unfortunate accident are asked to contact the police immediately.

Janet could scarcely believe what she had just read. She looked up into the smiling face of Louis who was watching her with interest.

"Wow! Now that's a shocker. Do you think we should contact the police and tell them what we know?"

Louis laughed. "I don't think that would be a good idea. You've been through enough in the last few months to last you a lifetime without having to add more. Let the cops do their job. I think they'll do just fine without our assistance. Besides, what can we tell them that would help? It sounds to me like old Ross was the architect of his own demise. And as far as I'm concerned, what happened to him is somehow poetic justice, wouldn't you say?"

Janet looked back down at the article, hardly able to get her mind around what had occurred to Ross. Did she feel sorry for him? Not at all. Perhaps she should have, she thought. After all, he was a human being and she had felt something for him at one point. But considering how miserable he had made her life, she found it difficult to shed a tear over him.

"It's a closed chapter in your life," Louis said. "There's no looking back now."

"You're probably right," Janet said. "I just can't help thinking –"

"If I were you, I wouldn't give it another thought. I know that will be hard, but you've got to put this thing behind you and get on with your life. You owe it to yourself and to your son."

Janet took a deep breath. "I guess you're right. I do deserve it. And so does Andrew."

The restaurant was beginning to get busy. Janet looked around. "Guess I better go and change before you fire me for dereliction of duty."

Louis laughed. "I think you should take this whole day off and celebrate your new life with your son. What do you think of that?"

Janet smiled up at her Guardian Angel. "You keep coming up with all these wonderful suggestions. I think I might just take you up on that."

CPSIA information can be obtained
at www.ICGtesting.com
Printed in the USA
LVOW11s0511061017
551419LV00001B/7/P

9 781773 701974